FIGHTIN'

FIGHTIN'

new and collected stories

by Simon J. Ortiz

Thunder's Mouth Press • Chicago • New York

Published in the United States by Thunder's Mouth Press, Box 780, NYC 10025; and Box 11223, Chicago 60611.

Design by Laurie Bolchert

Some of these stories have been previously published in the following publications: *New Mexico Quarterly*; *The Indian Speaks*; *The Man To Send Rainclouds*; *Howbah Indians*; *The Remembered Earth*; *Fight Back: For The Sake of The People, For The Sake of the Land*; *River Styx*; *Another Chicago Magazine* (ACM).

Grateful acknowledgment is made to the Illinois Arts Council and the National Endowment for the Arts for financial assistance with the publication of this volume.

Distributed by **Persea Books**, 225 Lafayette St., New York NY 10012

Library of Congress Cataloging in Publication Data

Ortiz, Simon J., 1941–
    Fightin': new and collected short stories.

    I. Title.
PS3565.R77F5   1983   813'.54   83-9196
ISBN 0-938410-15-6
ISBN 0-938410-14-8 (pbk.)

CONTENTS

Fightin'—we must. It's a struggle to live, to keep domestic harmony, to insure social, political, economic security, to maintain human integrity and dignity. We are faced constantly with small and large battles, some we know are battles, some we are unsure about. But we struggle in every case. Only by fightin', often fighting back, do we maintain a necessary vital life; this is our victory.

To Change In A Good Way

Bill and Ida lived in the mobile home park west of Milan. They'd come out with Kerr-McGee when the company first started sinking shafts at Ambrosia Lake. That would be in '58 or '59. He was an electrician's helper and Ida was a housewife though for a while she worked over at that 24-hour Catch-All store. But mostly she liked to be around home, the trailer park, and tried to plant a little garden on the little patch of clay land that came with the mobile home.

She missed Oklahoma like Bill did too. He always said they were going to just stay long enough to get a down payment, save enough, for some acreage in eastern Oklahoma around Eufala.

That's what he told Pete, the Laguna man he came to be friends with at Section 17. Pete worked as a lift operator, taking men into and out of the mine, and once in a while they worked the same shift and rode car pool together.

You're lucky you got some land, Pete, Bill would say.

It's not much but it's some land, Pete would agree.

He and Mary, his wife, had a small garden which they'd plant in the spring. Chili, couple rows of sweet corn, squash, beans, even had lettuce, cucumbers, and radishes, onions. They irrigated from the small stream, the Rio de San Jose, which runs through Acoma and Laguna land. Ida just had the clay red ground which she had planted that first spring they'd spent in New Mexico with lettuce and radishes and corn but the only thing that ever really came up was the corn and it was kind of stunted and wilty looking. She watered the little patch from the little green plastic hose hooked up to the town water system that started running dry about mid-June.

One Saturday, Pete and Mary and Bill and Ida were all shopping at the same time at the Sturgis Food Mart in Milan, and the women became friends too. They all went over to the mobile home park and sat around and drank pepsis and talked. Ida and Bill didn't have any kids but Mary and Pete had three.

They're at home, staying out of trouble I hope, Mary said.

Bill had a younger brother nicknamed Slick. He had a photo of him sitting on the TV stand shelf. Bill was proud of his little brother. He passed the photo to Pete and Mary. Slick was in the Army.

In Vietnam, Bill said, I worry about him some but at least he's learnt a trade. He's Spec-4 in Signal. Slick's been kind of wild, so I know about trouble.

Ida took Mary outside to show her her garden. It's kinda hard trying to grow anything here, Ida said, different from Oklahoma.

I think you need something in it, Ida, to break up the packed clay, Mary said. Maybe some sheep stuff. I'll tell Pete to bring you some.

The next weekend Pete brought some sheep stuff and spread it around the wilty plants. Work it around and into the ground, he said, but it'll be till next year that it will be better. He brought another pickup load later on.

Ida and Bill went down to Laguna too, to the reservation, and they met Pete and Mary's kids. Ida admired their small garden. Slick was visiting on leave and he came with them. He had re-upped, had a brand new Spec-5 patch on his shoulder and he had bought a motorcycle. He was on his way to another tour.

I wish he hadn't done that, Bill said. Folks at home are worried too. Good thing your boys aren't old enough.

In the yard, the kids, including Slick, were playing catch with a softball. He wasn't much older than Pete's and Mary's oldest. Slick had bright and playful eyes, handsome, and Bill was right to be proud of his kid brother.

I'm gonna make sure that young jackoff goes to college after the damn Army, Bill said.

After that, they'd visit each other. Ida would come help Mary with her garden. A couple times, the kids went to stay with Ida when Bill worked graveyard or swing because she didn't like to be alone. The kids liked that too, staying in town or what there was of it at the edge of Milan at the mobile home amidst others sitting on the clay hard ground. The clay had come around to being workable with the sheep stuff in it. Ida planted radishes and lettuce and carrots and corn, even tomatoes and chili, and she was so proud of her growing plants that summer.

One afternoon, up at Section 17, Bill got a message from the foreman to call Ida. They were underground replacing wire and he had to take the lift up. He called from the payphone outside the mine office.

Pete held the lift for him and when he came back Bill said, I gotta get my lunchpail and go home.

Something wrong, Bill? Pete asked. You okay?

Yeah, Bill said, something happened to Slick, the folks called from Claremore.

Hope it's not serious, Pete said.

On the way home after shift, Pete stopped at Bill's and Ida's. Ida answered the door and showed him in. Bill was sitting on the couch. He had a fifth of Heaven Hill halfway empty.

Pete, Bill said, Slick's gone. No more Slick. Got killed by stepping on a mine, an American mine—isn't that the shits, Pete? Dammit, Pete, just look at that kid.

He pointed at the photo on the TV stand.

Pete didn't say anything at first and then he said, Aamoo o dyumuu. And he put his arm around Bill's shoulders.

Bill poured him some Heaven Hill and Ida told him they were leaving for Claremore the next morning as soon as they could pack and the bank opened.

Should get there by evening, she said. And then Pete left.

When Pete got home, he told Mary what had happened.

Tomorrow morning on your way to work, drop me off there. I want to see Ida, Mary said.

You can go ahead and drive me to work and take the truck, Pete said.

That night they sat at the kitchen table with the kids and tied feathers and scraped cedar sticks and closed them in a cornhusk with cotton, beads, and tobacco. The next morning, Mary and Pete went by the mobile home park. Bill and Ida were loading the last of their luggage into their car.

After greetings and solaces, Mary said, We brought you some things. She gave Ida a loaf of Laguna bread. For your lunch, she said, and Ida put it in the ice chest.

Pete took a white corn ear and the cornhusk bundle out of a paper bag he carried, and he showed them to Bill. He said, This is just a corn, Bill, Indian corn. The people call it Kasheshi. Just a dried ear of corn. You can take it with you, or you can keep it here. You can plant it. It's to know that life will keep on, your life will keep on. Just like Slick will be planted again. He'll be like that, like seed planted, like corn seed, the Indian corn. But you and Ida, your life will grow on.

Pete put the corn ear back into the bag and then he held out the husk bundle. He said, I guess I don't remember some of what is done, Bill. Indian words, songs for it, what it all is, even how this is made just a certain way, but I know that it is important to do this. You take this too but you don't keep it. It's just for Slick, for his travel from this life among us to another place of being. You and Ida are not Indian, but it doesn't make any difference. It's for all of us, this kind of way, with corn and this, Bill. You take these sticks and feathers and you put them somewhere you think you should, somplace important that you think might be good, maybe to change life in a good way, that you think Slick would be helping us with.

You take it now, Pete said, and I know it may not sound easy to do but don't worry yourself too much. Slick is okay now, he'll be helping us, and you'll be fine too.

Pete put the paper bag in Bill's hand, and they all shook hands and hugged and Mary drove Pete on to Section 17.

After they left, Bill went inside their trailer home and took out the corn. He looked at it for a while, thinking, Just corn, just Indian corn, just your life to go on, Ida and you. And then he put the corn by the photo, by Slick on the TV stand. And then he wondered about the husk bundle. He couldn't figure it out. He couldn't figure it out. He'd grown up in Claremore all his life, Indians living all around him, folks and some school teachers said so, Cherokees in the Ozark hills, Creeks over to Muskogee, but Mary and Pete were the first Indians he'd ever known.

He held the bundle in his hand, thinking, and then he

decided not to take it to Oklahoma and put it in the cupboard. They locked up their mobile home and left.

Bill and Ida returned to Milan a week later. Most of the folks had been at the funeral and everything had gone alright. The folks were upset a whole lot but there wasn't much else to do except comfort them. Some of the other folks said that someone had to make the sacrifice for freedom of democracy and all that and that's what Slick had died of, for. He's done his duty for America, look at how much the past folks had to put up with, living a hard life, fighting off Indians to build homes on new land so we could live the way we are right now, advanced and safe from peril like the Tuls' Tribune said the other day Sunday that's what Slick died for, just like past folks.

That's what a couple relatives had advised and Bill tried to say what was bothering him, that the mine that Slick had stepped on was American and that the fact he was in a dangerous place was because he was in an Army that was American, and it didn't seem to be the same thing as what they were saying about past folks fighting Indians for democracy and it didn't seem right somehow.

But nobody really heard him; they just asked him about his job with Kerr-McGee, told him the company had built itself another building in Tulsa, Kerr's gonna screw those folks in New Mexico just like he has folks here being Senator. Ida and Bill visited for a while, comforted his folks for a while, and then they left for Milan.

By the time, they got back to their mobile home, Bill knew what he was going to do with the bundle of sticks and feathers. He'd been thinking about it all the way on I-40 from Oklahoma City, running it through his mind, what Slick had died of. Well, because of the bomb, stepping on the wrong place, being in a dangerous place, but something else. The reason was something else and though he wasn't completely sure about it yet he felt he was beginning to know. And he knew what he was going to do with the bundle in the cupboard.

The next morning, he put it in his lunchpail and went to work, reporting to the mine office first. He changed into his work clothes and put on his yellow slicker because they were going down that morning and he was glad for that for once. He took that paper bag out of his pail and put it in his overall pocket. After they went down he said he was going to go and check some cable and he made his way to the far end of a drift that had been mined out. He stopped and put the bundle down behind a slab of rock.

He didn't know what to do next and then he thought of what Pete had said. Say something about it.

Well, Bill thought, Slick, you was a good boy, kind of wild, but good. I got this here Indian thing, feathers and sticks, and at home, at home we got the corn by your picture, and Pete and Mary said to do this because it's important even if we're Okies and not Indians who do this. It's for your travel they said and to help us with our life here from where you are at now and they said to maybe change things in a good way for a good life and God knows us Okies always wanted that. Well, I'm gonna leave this here by the rock. Pete said he didn't know exactly all the right Indian things to do anymore but somehow I believe they're more righter than we've ever been led to believe. And now I'm trying too.

So you help us now, Slick. We need it, all the help we can get, even if it's just so much as holding up the roof of this mine that the damn company don't put enough timbers and bolts in, Bill said. And then he stepped back and left.

When Bill got home that evening, he told Ida what he had done, and she said, Next spring I'm gonna plant that Indian corn and Slick, if he's gonna help hold up the roof of Section 17, better be able to help with breaking up that clay dirt too.

Bill smiled and chuckled at Ida's remark. Nodding his head, he agreed.

Crossing

After five years in California, Charley Colorado was on his way back home to New Mexico. He had stopped to visit with his sister, Dianne, who lived in Palo Alto.

"Five years," he said, "I don't know what I expected but I don't have much to show for having come to California."

It was late afternoon, and they had been talking for a long time in Dianne's apartment. It was different now—that much was certain. Dianne was finishing law school and he had worked in San Francisco for five years. Indians were places they had never been; they were doing things they hadn't done before. They had talked about that, had even agreed on the certainty, and now they had grown quiet.

After a while, Charley picked up a photograph from a TV stand. He turned it over and read, Charles and Dianne 1961.

"I didn't know you had this. Do you remember where the photograph was taken?" Charley asked.

"It was in southern California where Dad was working. Mama, you and I went to visit him that summer. You were in your first year of Indian School," Dianne said.

"We went by train," Charley said. "Dad met us in Barstow and we stayed with relatives at the Indian Colony. Next day, we went where the track gang was, near San Clemente. You and I wanted to see the ocean right away, and we all walked down to the beach. I was so excited and scared when the ocean came into view. It took my breath away."

"You look so serious in the picture, Charley," Dianne said. "Just like you look now." She laughed.

Charley laughed too. "I was scared. I didn't like where Dad lived, that box bunk car. The whole thing would shake whenever a train passed by on the next track."

"We didn't stay there long,"Dianne said. "We went back to the Indian Colony. Such a name, but that's what it was. The railroad company brought Indian people from New Mexico and put them in little firetrap houses on company owned land by the railroad yards."

The brother and sister both knew very certainly what had happened. After the railroad had taken the very best lands along the river in the 1890's, Indians couldn't make a living from the land they had left. So they took jobs on the railroad in meager compensation.

"Daddy would come home from laying track, and he would be all grimy and exhausted, groaning from pained muscles. It's no wonder he and other men drank until they couldn't feel anything."

Charley would be dismayed. His father's speech would slur and he would stumble around when he was usually so graceful. Drunkenness was common at the Colony; there were always fights, there was always screaming. He would hide everytime his father and the other men got drunk. At the Indian Colony, he would see the men trudging off to work in the mornings and returning in the evenings looking like they had just lost a battle.

"Do you remember that story Grandpa Santiago would tell? It was after the railroad came. Things had become so poor, the people were sick, there wasn't much to eat. There was little useful land left. The men decided to leave the Pueblo to find work." Dianne was simply stating a fact and a rememberance told by their grandfather when they were children.

"He said, 'The men packed provisions for a long journey on burros and horses. Some men had neither so they were to take turns riding and walking. I was this tall, just a small boy. There was a great flurry of activity and apprehension for who knew what might happen—there were unforeseen events and even danger. But being very young, I found it of great excitement. There was weeping upon the leave-taking. Wives, mothers, sons, daughters, beloved ones were crying and calling to them— Be well, avoid danger, come back; may fortune and the guiding spirits of our people be with you. They left singing this song:

Kalrrahuurrniah ah
Kalrrahuurrniah ah
Steh ehyuu uuh.

From the edge of the Pueblo, our homeland, we watched them until they disappeared into the west.' "

Yes, Charley remembered clearly the old man speaking; his voice had been somewhat sad but always resolute, knowing what had happened. 'There was an old old woman who could not see very well, who kept looking to the west long long after the men had left. She kept murmuring prayers and saying, Tell the rain to come, young men. When you meet the clouds at the western edge, tell them we need their help. Bring the rain home with you, young men, from that great water. Your journey will be for all of us, young men, and for the land. And she sang. My brother and I sat with the old woman until it was too dark to see anything but the faint light over the mountains and a few red clouds. I imagined it was dust clouds being raised by the burros and men.'

"Those men from the Pueblo decided to do what was necessary," Dianne said. "There was nothing else they could do; they had to try. It may sound odd, but they were like the Okies who, later on, came to California. What land they had left was worthless. No living could be made off it; the Okies couldn't either. It wasn't only the duststorms, like some historians would have us believe. The people were being forced off the land."

Charley had asked his mother for details of the journey taken by the men. She told him, It happened that they arrived at a big river after they had travelled for many days. At the river, they were stopped by men who demanded payment for crossing the river which was a border. The men had guns and they told our beloved men they could cross only if they made payment for passage on a boat.

The men didn't have any money. All they had was the desire to work; that's why they had made the decision to go to California. So they didn't know what to do at first. Some wanted to cross at another place but others said it would be dangerous. There were men with guns on the other side of the river who would demand paper evidence of having paid for crossing. Some men said it was fruitless to go on and they wanted to go home.

We all have to be of one mind and purpose and we all have to decide, the leaders said. We came on this journey to find work because we have the ability and the desire to work, but it is obvious these people here will not let us pass without payment and they have said they do not want more Indians in their state anyway. But we have a purpose, to help our people who are suffering a difficult time—remember them. So the men, beloved, decided to sell what possessions they had, their burros and horses and even their weapons, in order to pay for the passage of several of their number.

It must have been a sad time, Charley's mother said. When the men who couldn't cross returned home, they almost had nothing left. It was about 1911, and it was a dim and hard time for our people then.

Dianne said to Charley, "For a long time, I thought the story was kind of sad because most of the men didn't get to California and they returned with nothing. But then, thinking about it, it's not sad. The men decided what to do. They sold everything in order to have a few go on. They didn't just turn back. A few would make that crossing for whatever it meant—to make a living, to summon the rain from the ocean—just as they had all set out to do. I only heard Santiago tell the story when we were children but I remember every detail."

The next morning came with the sunlight streaming through thin curtains unto the red carpet of Dianne's apartment. For several moments, Charley, lying face down on the edge of the sofa bed made up for him by his sister, could not shake the dream that was happening. First One was shouting, Come, hurry, we're almost there!

He could barely hear the shout as it came from a vast distance across a valley. And the valley was filled with a furious molten motion of lava which hissed, and sputtered, and leaped up in rippling surges.

He, the Second One, was afraid and he trembled. First One called again. Even at the distance, Second One could see that where his brother was it was green, lush with grass, and the land above and beyond him was filled with tall trees. And above the trees and beyond were clouds, white and thick rain clouds.

They had been sent to take word to the rain clouds. But his fear froze him to the ground, and he could not move. The very ground, rocky and barren, he stood upon shook with the surging of the molten rock. He was desperate; he did not want to fail; the people were waiting for the rain.

Faintly, across the vast fearsome valley, he heard his brother's voice call, "Look behind you!"

He looked and there was nothing but barren rocky hills and dried tree trunks and beyond that the flat white sky. What was he to see? he moaned with a parched throat. And then in the distance, indistinct at first, coming very slowly, was someone. His eyes burning, he strained to see who it was.

It was an old woman with white hair, painfully making her way among huge boulders in her way, and she was blind. Without thinking, Second One ran to her and said, Grandmother, there is danger ahead, you should not be walking towards it: turn back. And the old woman looked at him with her white-turned eyes and said, Grandson, I have come to help you on your mission to help the people and the land.

She was so old even her words were slow, and she put her hand in an apron pocket and brought out a flowered handkerchief. Untying the knot, she showed him a white stone nestled in cornmeal, and she drew the stone out and handed it to him.

Take this, she said, tie it to your arrow and let it fly across to the other side. She took the cornmeal and breathing upon it all around in a circle to the horizons, she sprinkled it on the ground and shook out her handkerchief.

He did as he was told, quickly tied the stone to the arrow-shaft with sinew, and then pulling on his bow with all his might, he let the arrow fly. It flew until he lost sight of it and suddenly in the path of its flight appeared a silver thread arcing above the ferocious valley of lava.

Quickly, Grandson, the old woman said, go as fast as you can. Don't worry, it will hold you.

Calling, "Thank you, Grandmother," he stepped on the thread and ran as fast as he could. From below, he could feel the furious red heat leaping up to his face.

Charley shook his head and squinted his eyes at the morning light falling on his face and the carpet. "Thank you," he said quietly. "All around and beyond, thank you, for the journey here and for the journey home to the Pueblo and for the crossing, thank you."

Men on the Moon

Joselita brought her father, Faustin, the TV on Father's Day. She brought it over after Sunday mass and she had her son hook up the antenna. She plugged the TV into the wall socket.

Faustin sat on a worn couch. He was covered with an old coat. He had worn that coat for twenty years.

It's ready. Turn it on and I'll adjust the antenna, Amarosho told his mother. The TV warmed up and then it flickered into dull light. It was snowing. Amarosho tuned it a bit. It snowed less and then a picture formed.

Look, Naishtiya, Joselita said. She touched her father's hand and pointed at the TV.

I'll turn the antenna a bit and you tell me when the picture is clear, Amarosho said. He climbed on the roof again.

After a while the picture turned clearer. It's better, his mother shouted. There was only the tiniest bit of snow falling.

That's about the best it can get I guess, Amarosho said. Maybe it'll clear up on the other channels. He turned the selector. It was clearer on another.

There were two men struggling with each other. Wrestling, Amarosho said. Do you want to watch wrestling? Two men are fighting, Nana. One of them is Apache Red. Chiseh tsah, he told his grandfather.

The old man stirred. He had been staring intently into the TV. He wondered why there was so much snow at first. Now there were two men fighting. One of them was Chiseh, an Apache, and the other was a Mericano. There were people shouting excitedly and clapping hands within the TV.

The two men backed away from each other once in a while and then they clenched. They wheeled mightily and suddenly one threw the other. The old man smiled. He wondered why they were fighting.

Something else showed on the TV screen. A bottle of wine

was being poured. The old man liked the pouring sound and he moved his mouth. Someone was selling wine.

The two fighting men came back on the TV. They struggled with each and after a while one of them didn't get up and then another person came and held up the hand of the Apache who was dancing around in a feathered headdress.

It's over, Amarosho announced. Apache Red won the fight, Nana.

The Chisheh won. Faustin watched the other one, a light-haired man who looked totally exhausted and angry with himself. He didn't like the Apache too much. He wanted them to fight again.

After a few moments something else appeared on the TV.

What is that? Faustin asked. There was an object with smoke coming from it. It was standing upright.

Men are going to the moon, Nana, his grandson said. It's Apollo. It's going to fly three men to the moon.

That thing is going to fly to the moon?

Yes, Nana.

What is it called again?

Apollo, a spaceship rocket, Joselita told her father.

The Apollo spaceship stood on the ground emitting clouds of something that looked like smoke.

A man was talking, telling about the plans for the flight, what would happen, that it was almost time. Faustin could not understand the man very well because he didn't know many words in Mericano.

He must be talking about that thing flying in the air? he said.

Yes. It's about ready to fly away to the moon.

Faustin remembered that the evening before he had looked at the sky and seen that the moon was almost in the middle phase. He wondered if it was important that the men get to the moon.

Are those men looking for something on the moon? he asked his grandson.

They're trying to find out what's on the moon, Nana, what kind of dirt and rocks there are, to see if there's any life on the moon. The men are looking for knowledge, Amarosho told him.

Faustin wondered if the men had run out of places to look for knowledge on the earth. Do they know if they'll find knowledge? he asked.

They have some information already. They've gone before and come back. They're going again.

Did they bring any back?

They brought back some rocks.

Rocks. Faustin laughed quietly. The scientist men went to search for knowledge on the moon and they brought back rocks. He thought that perhaps Amarosho was joking with him. The grandson had gone to Indian School for a number of years and sometimes he would tell his grandfather some strange and funny things.

The old man was suspicious. They joked around a lot. Rocks—you sure that's all they brought back?

That's right, Nana, only rocks and some dirt and pictures they made of what it looks like on the moon.

The TV picture was filled with the rocket, close up now. Men were sitting and moving around by some machinery and the voice had become more urgent. The old man watched the activity in the picture intently but with a slight smile on his face.

Suddenly it became very quiet, and the voice was firm and commanding and curiously pleading. Ten, nine, eight, seven, six, five, four, three, two, liftoff. The white smoke became furious and a muted rumble shook through the TV. The rocket was trembling and the voice was trembling.

It was really happening, the old man marvelled. Somewhere inside of that cylinder with a point at its top and long slender wings were three men who were flying to the moon.

The rocket rose from the ground. There were enormous clouds of smoke and the picture shook. Even the old man became tense and he grasped the edge of the couch. The rocket spaceship rose and rose.

There's fire coming out of the rocket, Amarosho explained. That's what makes it go.

Fire. Faustin had wondered what made it fly. He'd seen pictures of other flying machines. They had long wings and someone had explained to him that there was machinery inside which spun metal blades which made them fly. He had wondered what made this thing fly. He hoped his grandson wasn't joking him.

After a while there was nothing but the sky. The rocket Apollo had disappeared. It hadn't taken very long and the voice from the TV wasn't excited anymore. In fact the voice was very calm and almost bored.

I have to go now, Naishtiya, Joselita told her father. I have things to do.

Me too, Amarosho said.

Wait, the old man said, wait. What shall I do with this thing. What is it you call it?

TV, his daughter said. You watch it. You turn it on and you watch it.

I mean how do you stop it. Does it stop like the radio, like the mahkina? It stops?

This way, Nana, Amarosho said and showed his grandfather. He turned the dial and the picture went away. He turned the dial again and the picture flickered on again. Were you afraid this one-eye would be looking at you all the time? Amarosho laughed and gently patted the old man's shoulder.

Faustin was relieved. Joselita and her son left. He watched the TV for a while. A lot of activity was going on, a lot of men were moving among machinery, and a couple of men were talking. And then it showed the rocket again.

He watched it rise and fly away again. It disappeared again. There was nothing but the sky. He turned the dial and the picture died away. He turned it on and the picture came on again. He turned it off. He went outside and to a fence a distance from his home. When he finished he studied the sky for a while.

II.

That night, he dreamed.

Flintwing Boy was watching a Skquuyuh mahkina come down a hill. The mahkina made a humming noise. It was walking. It shone in the sunlight. Flintwing Boy moved to a better position to see. The mahkina kept on moving. It was moving towards him.

The Skquuyuh mahkina drew closer. Its metal legs stepped

upon trees and crushed growing flowers and grass. A deer bounded away frightened. Tshushki came running to Flintwing Boy.

Anaweh, he cried, trying to catch his breath.

The coyote was staring at the thing which was coming towards them. There was wild fear in his eyes.

What is that, Anaweh? What is that thing? he gasped.

It looks like a mahkina, but I've never seen one like it before. It must be some kind of Skquuyuh mahkina.

Where did it come from?

I'm not sure yet, Anaweh, Flintwing Boy said. When he saw that Tshushki was trembling with fear, he said gently, Sit down, Anaweh. Rest yourself. We'll find out soon enough.

The Skquuyuh mahkina was undeterred. It walked over and through everything. It splashed through a stream of clear water. The water boiled and streaks of oil flowed downstream. It split a juniper tree in half with a terrible crash. It crushed a boulder into dust with a sound of heavy metal. Nothing stopped the Skquuyuh mahkina. It hummed.

Anaweh, Tshushki cried, what shall we do? What can we do?

Flintwing Boy reached into the bag at his side. He took out an object. It was a flint arrowhead. He took out some cornfood.

Come over here, Anaweh. Come over here. Be calm, he motioned to the frightened coyote. He touched the coyote in several places of his body with the arrowhead and put cornfood in the palm of his hand.

This way, Flintwing Boy said and closed Tshshki's fingers over the cornfood gently. And they faced east. Flintwing Boy said, We humble ourselves again. We look in your direction for guidance. We ask for your protection. We humble our poor bodies and spirits because only you are the power and the source and the knowledge. Help us then—that is all we ask.

They breathed on the cornfood and took in the breath of all directions and gave the cornfood unto the ground.

Now the ground trembled with the awesome power of the Skquuyuh mahkina. Its humming vibrated against everything. Flintwing Boy reached behind him and took several arrows from his quiver. He inspected them carefully and without any rush he fit one to his bowstring.

And now, Anaweh, you must go and tell everyone. Describe what you have seen. The people must talk among themselves and decide what it is about and what they will do. You must hurry but you must not alarm the people. Tell them I am here to meet it. I will give them my report when I find out.

Coyote turned and began to run. He stopped several yards away. Hahtrudzaimeh, he called. Like a man of courage, Anaweh, like a man.

The old man stirred in his sleep. A dog was barking. He awoke and got out of his bed and went outside. The moon was past the midpoint and it would be morning light in a few hours.

III.

Later, the spaceship reached the moon.

Amarosho was with his grandfather. They watched a replay of two men walking on the moon.

So that's the men on the moon, Faustin said.

Yes, Nana, that's it.

There were two men inside of heavy clothing and equipment. The TV picture showed a closeup of one of them and indeed there was a man's face inside of glass. The face moved its mouth and smiled and spoke but the voice seemed to be separate from the face.

It must be cold. They have heavy clothing on, Faustin said.

It's supposed to be very cold and very hot. They wear the clothes and other things for protection from the cold and heat, Amarosho said.

The men on the moon were moving slowly. One of them skipped and he floated alongside the other.

The old man wondered if they were underwater. They seem to be able to float, he said.

The information I have heard is that a man weighs less than he does on earth, much less, and he floats. There is no air either to breathe. Those boxes on their backs contain air for them to breathe, Amarosho told his grandfather.

He weighs less, the old man wondered, and there is no air except for the boxes on their backs. He looked at Amarosho but his grandson didn't seem to be joking with him.

The land on the moon looked very dry. It looked like it had not rained for a long, long time. There were no trees, no plants, no grass. Nothing but dirt and rocks, a desert.

Amarosho had told him that men on earth—the scientists—believed there was no life on the moon. Yet those men were trying to find knowledge on the moon. He wondered if perhaps they had special tools with which they could find knowledge even if they believed there was no life on the moon desert.

The mahkina sat on the desert. It didn't make a sound. Its metal feet were planted flat on the ground. It looked somewhat awkward. Faustin searched vainly around the mahkina but there didn't seem to be anything except the dry land on the TV. He couldn't figure out the mahkina. He wasn't sure whether it could move and could cause fear. He didn't want to ask his grandson that question.

After a while, one of the bulky men was digging in the ground. He carried a long thin hoe with which he scooped dirt and put it into a container. He did this for a while.

Is he going to bring the dirt back to earth too? Faustin asked.

I think he is, Nana, Amarosho said. Maybe he'll get some rocks too. Watch.

Indeed several minutes later the man lumbered over to a pile of rocks and gathered several handsize ones. He held them out proudly. They looked just like rocks from around anyplace. The voice from the TV seemed to be excited about the rocks.

They will study the rocks too for knowledge?

Yes, Nana.

What will they use the knowledge for, Nana?

They say they will use it to better mankind, Nana. I've heard that. And to learn more about the universe we live in. Also some of them say that the knowledge will be useful in finding out where everything began and how everything was made.

Faustin smiled at his grandson. He said, You are telling me the true facts aren't you?

Why yes, Nana. That's what they say. I'm not just making it up, Amarosho said.

Well then—do they say why they need to know where everything began? Hasn't anyone ever told them?

I think other people have tried to tell them but they want to find out for themselves and also I think they claim they don't know enough and need to know more and for certain, Amarosho said.

The man in the bulky suit had a small pickaxe in his hand. He was striking at a boulder. The breathing of the man could clearly be heard. He seemed to be working very hard and was very tired.

Faustin had once watched a crew of Mericano drilling for water. They had brought a tall mahkina with a loud motor. The mahkina would raise a limb at its center to its very top and then drop it with a heavy and loud metal clang. The mahkina and its men sat at one spot for several days and finally they found water.

The water had bubbled out weakly, gray-looking and didn't look drinkable at all. And then they lowered the mahkina, put their equipment away and drove away. The water stopped flowing.

After a couple of days he went and checked out the place. There was nothing there except a pile of gray dirt and an indentation in the ground. The ground was already dry and there were dark spots of oil-soaked dirt.

He decided to tell Amarosho about the dream he had.

After the old man finished, Amarosho said, Old man, you're telling me the truth now? You know that you have become somewhat of a liar. He was teasing his grandfather.

Yes, Nana. I have told you the truth as it occurred to me that night. Everything happened like that except that I might not have recalled everything about it.

That's some story, Nana, but it's a dream.

It's a dream but it's the truth, Faustin said.

I believe you, Nana, his grandson said.

Sometime after that the spacemen returned to earth. Amarosho informed his grandfather that they had splashed down in the ocean.

Are they all right? Faustin asked.

Yes, Amarosho said. They have devices to keep them safe.

Are they in their homes now?

No, I think they have to be someplace where they can't contaminate anything. If they brought back something from the moon that they weren't supposed to they won't pass it on to somebody else, Amarosho said.

What would that something be?

Something harmful, Nana.

In that dry desert land there might be something harmful. I didn't see any strange insects or trees or even cactus. What would that harmful thing be, Nana?

Disease which might harm people on earth, Amarosho said.

You said there was the belief by the men that there is no life on the moon. Is there life after all? Faustin asked.

There might be the tiniest bit of life.

Yes I see now, Nana. If they find even the tiniest bit of life then they will believe, he said.

Yes. Something like that.

Faustin figured it out now. The men had taken that trip to the moon to find even the tiniest bit of life and if they found even the tiniest bit they would believe that they had found knowledge. Yes that must be the way it was.

He remembered his dream clearly now. He was relieved.

When are those two men fighting again, Nana? he asked his grandson.

What two men?

Those two men who were fighting with each other that day those other men were flying to the moon.

Oh—those men. I don't know, Nana. Maybe next Sunday. You like them?

Yes. I think that the next time I'll be cheering for the Apache. He'll win again. He'll beat the Mericano again, Faustin said, laughing.

Woman Singing

"Yessir, pretty good stuff," Willie said. He handed the bottle of Thunderbird wine to Clyde.

Clyde took a drink and then another before he said anything. He looked out the window of their wooden shack. Gray and brown land outside. Snow soon, but hope not, Clyde thought.

"Yes," Clyde said. But he didn't like it. He didn't drink wine very much, maybe some sometimes, but none very much.

Willie reached for the bottle, and Clyde thought that Willie didn't mind drinking anything. Any wine was just another drink. But he knew, too, that Willie liked whiskey, and he liked beer too. It didn't make any difference to Willie. Clyde wished he had some beer.

They had come from the potato fields a few minutes before. It was cold outside and Willie threw some wood into the kitchen stove as soon as they came in. He poured in kerosene from a mason jar and threw in a match. After a moment, the kerosene caught the small fire and exploded with a muffled sound. Willie jumped back and laughed. Clyde hung up his coat and then put it back on when he saw there were only a few pieces of wood in the woodbox. He looked over at Willie, but Willie was taking his coat off and so Clyde went on out to get the wood. Willie didn't do anything he didn't have to.

There was singing from the shack across from theirs. Singing, The People singing, Clyde said to himself in his native Indian tongue. It was a woman. Sad kind of, but not lonely, just something which bothered him, made him think of Arizona, his homeland. Brown and red land. Pinon, yucca, and his father's sheep, the dogs too around the door of the hogan at evening. Smoke and smell of stew and bread, and the older smell of the juniper mingled with the sheep. His heart and thoughts were lonely. Woman singing, The People singing, here and now,

Clyde thought to himself. He stood for a while and listened and then looked over at the shack. The door was tightly shut, but the walls were thin, just scrap lumber and roofing paper, and the woman's voice was almost clear. Clyde was tempted to approach the shack and listen closer, his loneliness now pressed him, but he would not because it was broad daylight and it was not the way to do things. The woman was Joe Shorty's wife, and she was the mother of two children. Clyde picked up an armful of wood and returned to his own shack.

"Have some more, son," Willie said. Willie was only a few years older than Clyde, but he called him son sometimes. Just for fun, and Clyde would call him father in return. Willie was married and the father of two children. They lived in New Mexico while he worked in the Idaho potato fields.

"I think I'll fix us something to eat." Clyde said after he had taken a drink. He began to peel some potatoes. Willie's going to get drunk again, he thought. Yessir. They had gotten paid, and Willie had been fidgety since morning when they had received their money from Wheeler, their boss. He had told the Indians who worked for him, "Now I know that some of you are leaving as soon as you get paid, well that's okay with me because they ain't much to do around here until next year. But some of you are staying for a while longer, and I'm telling those guys who are staying that they better stay sober. Besides, it's getting colder out, and we don't want no froze Indians around." Wheeler laughed, and Willie laughed with him. Clyde didn't like the boss, and he didn't look at him or say anything when he received his pay. He was going to stay for at least another month, but he didn't want to. But he figured he had to since he wasn't sure whether he could get a job around home right off or even at all. Willie was staying too, because he didn't feel like going home just yet, besides the fact that his family needed money.

"I think I'm gonna go to town tonight," Willie said. He was casual in saying it, but he was excited and he had been planning for it since morning. "Joe Shorty and his wife are coming along. You want to come?"

"I'm not sure," Clyde said. He didn't know Joe Shorty too well, and he had only said Hello to his wife and children.

"Come on," Willie insisted. "We'll go to a show and then to

the Elkhorn Bar. Dancing there. And all the drunks have left, so it'll be okay now. Come with us."

"Yeah, I might," Clyde said. He listened for the woman's singing while they ate, but the fire crackling in the stove was loud and Willie kept talking about going to town. "Isn't Joe Shorty and his family going back home?" Clyde asked.

"I don't know," Willie answered. He pushed back his chair and carried the dishes to the sink. Clyde began to wash the dishes but Willie stopped him. "Come on, let's go."

When they knocked on Joe Shorty's door, a boy answered. He looked at the two men and then ran back inside. Joe came to the door.

"Okay, just a little while," Joe said.

Willie and Clyde sat on the front step. They could hear movement and mumbled talk inside. Clyde thought about the singing woman. He felt uncomfortable because he was thinking of another man's woman. It was a healing song, strong mountains in it, strong and sharp and clear, and far up. Women always make songs strong, he thought. He almost told Willie about the song.

Joe and his wife and children, two boys, came out and they all began to walk on the road towards town. It was five miles away, and usually someone was driving into town and would give them a ride. If not, they would walk all the way. The children ran and walked ahead. They talked quietly with each other, but the grownups didn't say anything.

When they had walked a mile, a pickup truck stopped for them. It was Wheeler. "Hey, Willie. Everybody going to town, huh? Come," Wheeler called.

Willie and Clyde got in front with Wheeler, and Joe and his family got in the back.

"Well, gonna go have a good time, huh? Drink and raise hell," Wheeler said loudly and laughed. He punched Willie in the side playfully. He drove pretty fast along the gravel road.

Willie smiled. The wine he had finished off was warm in him. He wished he had another bottle. Out of the corners of his eyes, he searched the cab, and wondered if Wheeler might have a drink to offer.

"You Indians are the best damn workers," Wheeler said.

"And I don't mind giving you a ride in my truck. Place down the road's got a bunch of Mexicans, had them up at my place several years back, but they ain't no good. Lazier than any Indian anytime, them Mexicans are. Couldn't nothing move them once they sit down. But you people—and for this reason I don't mind giving you a lift to town—Willie and your friend there do your work when I tell you, and that means you're okay for my farm."

Clyde felt the wine move in his belly. It made him swallow and he turned his head a little and saw that the woman's scarf had fallen away from her head. She was trying to put it back on.

"That Joe's got a pretty woman," Wheeler said to Willie. He looked at Clyde for comment, but Clyde would not look at him. Willie smiled and nodded.

"Yeah, don't get to see too many pretty Indian women around the camps, but she's a pretty one. You think so, Willie?" Wheeler nudged Willie with his elbow.

"Yes," Willie said and he shrunk down in his seat. He wished Wheeler would offer him a drink if he had any. But he knew that he probably wouldn't.

"Hey, Clyde, you married? A woman at home?" Wheeler asked, but he didn't look at Clyde. They were approaching the town and Clyde stared straight ahead at it but he decided to answer.

"No," Clyde said. "Not yet, maybe when I get enough money." He smiled faintly to show that he was making a minor joke.

"Someday you'll get a woman, maybe a pretty one like Joe's, with or without money," Wheeler said. And he laughed loudly. He pulled the pickup truck over to a curb in the center of the small town. "Well, take it easy. Don't overdo it. Or else you'll land in jail or freeze out in the cold or something," Wheeler said with no special concern.

"We're going to the show," Willie said, and he smiled at Wheeler.

"Okay," Wheeler said, gave a quick laugh, and turned to watch Joe's wife climb out of the truck. He wanted to catch her eye, maybe to wink at her, but she didn't look at him. He watched the Indians walk up the street towards the town theater. The woman and her children followed behind the men.

Wheeler thought about all the drunk Indians he'd seen in his life. He shrugged his shoulders and turned down the street in the opposite direction.

The movie was about a singer. Hank Williams was the singer's name. Clyde knew who he was, used to be on the Grand Ole Opry on radio, he remembered, sang songs he remembered too. Clyde thought about the singers back home. The singers of the land, the people, the rain, the good things of his home. His uncle on his mother's side was a medicine man, and he used to listen to him sing. In the quiet and cold winter evenings, lying on his sheepskin beside the fire, he would listen and sing under his breath with his uncle. Sing with me, his uncle would say, and Clyde would sing. But he had a long ways to go in truly learning the songs; he could not sing many of them and could only remember the feeling of them.

Willie laughed at the funny incidents in the movie, and he laughed about the drunk Hank Williams. That made him wish he had a drink again, and he tried to persuade Joe to go with him, but Joe didn't want to leave. Joe's wife and children watched the movie and the people around them, and they watched Willie fidget around in his seat. They figured he wanted to go drink.

At the end of the movie, they walked to a small cafe. On the way Willie ran into a liquor store and bought a pint of whiskey.

"Come on, son," he said to Clyde. "Help your father drink this medicine." Joe followed along into an alley where they quickly gulped some of the liquor.

"Call your woman and ask if she wants some," Willie said to Joe. He was in good spirit now. The whiskey ran through him quickly and lightly.

"Emma, come here," Joe called to his wife. She hesitated, looked up the street, and stepped into the alley. Her husband handed her the bottle and she drank quickly. She coughed and gasped for a moment, and Willie and Joe laughed.

Clyde saw the two children watching them. They stood in the weak overhead glare of a streetlight. Traffic barely moved, and a few people from the movies were walking on the streets. The children waited patiently for their parents.

They ate a quick dinner of hamburgers and cokes. And

when they finished, they paid up and walked to the Elkhorn Bar a couple of blocks away.

"Do se doe," Willie said when he heard the music coming from the bar. Saturday night was always a busy night, but most of the Indian potato pickers were gone now. There were only a few cars and trucks; some men and women stood by the door. A small fire blazed several yards from the bar, and around it were a few Indians quietly talking.

Willie walked over to the fire, and Clyde followed him because he didn't want to be left alone. Joe and his family stood beside the door of the bar and peered in.

"Here comes a drunk," someone in the circle of Indians said as Willie and Clyde walked up. They laughed, but it was not meant in harm. For a moment, as he did upon entering a crowd away from his home, Clyde felt a small tension, but he relaxed quickly and he talked with an acquaintance. Willie passed him a bottle, and he made a small joke, and Clyde laughed. He felt better and took a long drink. Whiskey went down into the belly harder than wine but it made him feel warmer. And when he thought that it didn't make any difference to Willie what he drank he laughed to himself. The men talked.

The talk was mostly about their home and about The People at home. Clyde again felt the thought travel into his heart. It made him long for his home. He didn't belong here even though he had friends here, and he had money in his pocket and a job. He was from another place, where his people came from and belonged. Yet here some of them were around this fire, outside the Elkhorn Bar, and they worked in the Idaho potato fields cultivating, irrigating, and picking potatoes. Someone began a song. It was the season for songs back in The People's land. The song was about a moving People.

When no one passed a bottle for a while, Clyde decided to go get a drink at the bar. The liquor in him made him sleepy, but he was getting cold too. There was no wind, but it was getting colder. He remembered Wheeler's words, thought about them for a moment, but he knew it would not freeze tonight. The bar was crowded. Someone was on the floor near the doorway, and others stepped over him without taking much notice.

Clyde met Joe Shorty and his wife, and they drank some

without him. Clyde didn't want to talk with them because they were another man's wife and children. They heard him and one of the boys said loudly, "It's Clyde. Clyde, come walk with us."

The woman was slightly drunk. Clyde could see her smile. She staggered some. "It's cold," she said. "We left Joe Shorty. He's going to come home in the morning."

Joe Shorty's wife and sons and Clyde walked quietly and steadily. The children stepped carefully in the dark. Once, Clyde looked back, and he could barely make out a pale light over the town. He thought about Willie and thought he would be all right. It was cold and Clyde let his hand out of his pocket to test the cold. Willie would be all right. Joe Shorty and Willie would probably come back to the camp together in the morning.

The lights of a truck lit them up and Clyde said, "We better get on this side of the road." The younger boy stumbled and grabbed for Clyde's hand. The boy's hand was cold, and Clyde felt funny with Joe Shorty's son's hand in his.

The truck was Wheeler's. It passed them and then slowed to a stop fifty yards ahead. Wheeler honked his horn. Clyde and Joe Shorty's family walked toward the truck as it backed towards them.

"It's Wheeler, the potato boss," Clyde said to the woman. She did not look at him or say anything. The younger boy clung to his mother's skirt.

The pickup truck drew back alongside of them and stopped. Wheeler rolled down his window and studied them for a moment. He looked at Clyde and winked. Clyde felt a small panic begin in him. He realized that he still held the child's hand in his. What did this mean to the potato boss, Clyde asked himself.

"Well come on," Wheeler said. "Get in, but just a minute," and he got out. He stood by the side of the truck and urinated. The woman and her children and then Clyde climbed into the back of the truck.

When Wheeler saw that they had climbed in back, he said gruffly, "Come on, get in front." And then with a softer tone, "There's enough room and it's colder than hell out," and he reached out a hand to one of the boys. But the boy hung back. Wheeler grabbed the other and swung him over the side. The woman and the other boy had no choice but to follow.

beer together. Joe was getting drunk and his wife was drinking quietly. It was too noisy for Clyde to remember the song anymore. The children were standing by the jukebox, watching the revolving discs. Clyde wondered when they were going back to the camp by the potato fields, and he went to look for Willie.

"So there you are, son," Willie said when Clyde found him. He was drunk, and he handed Clyde another bottle.

The Indians, who were very few now, were singing in the high voice of The People. Like the wind blowing through clefts in the mountains. Clyde wondered if it was only that he was getting drunk with the liquor that he could make out the wind and the mountains in the song. But it was the men getting drunk too, which didn't make it sound like the wind, he thought. He drank some more, but he was getting tired and colder, and he told Willie he wanted to go.

"No, stay," Willie said. "It is still a long night. These nights are long, and at home the sings last all night long."

This Idaho was not where The People's home was, Clyde thought. And he wanted to tell Willie that. He wanted to tell the others that, but they wouldn't pay attention to him, he knew.

The women would sit or stand quietly by the singing men at home. The fire would be big, and when it got smaller someone would bring an armload of wood and throw it in. Children would hurry through the crowd of The People until they were tired and sleepy. Here there were no children except by the jukebox, watching it play records. In the morning, there would be newly built fires before camps of families. In the mountains of The People. And the light beginning in the East would show that maybe it will snow sometime soon, but here by the Elkhorn Bar there would be no fires and no one to see the light in the East. Maybe, like Wheeler talked, there'd be some frozen Indian left lying around.

Clyde walked away. The town was quiet. A police cruiser went in the direction of the bar and the officer looked at Clyde. When he got to the edge of town, he lengthened his stride.

When he had walked for a while, he saw that someone was walking in front of him. He slowed down, and he saw that it was a woman and two children. Joe Shorty's family. Joe must have stayed, drunk I guess, Clyde thought, and his family had left

Clyde felt his feelings empty for a while and then he slowly felt himself burning. He watched the woman climb out of the back into the front. It was not cold as before and it was the liquor, he thought. When he jumped down from the back and got into the front he felt light and springy. He smiled at Wheeler.

Joe Shorty's wife did not say anything. She was looking at the dashboard and her children huddled against her.

"Well, Joe Shorty must be having a good time," Wheeler said. He laughed and steered wildly to keep the truck on the road.

The woman did not say anything. She held one of her children, and the other huddled against her tightly. Clyde was on the side against the door. He could feel her movement and her warmth. But he looked straight ahead until Wheeler spoke to him.

"Weren't you having a good time, Clyde? Maybe there's good times other places, huh?"

Clyde felt a hot liquid move in him. It was warm in the truck. The heater was blowing on his ankles. It's the whiskey, he thought. What does this man think of this, he thought. And then he thought of what all the white men in the world thought about all the Indians in the world. I'm drunk, he thought, and he wanted to sing that in his own language, The People's language, but there didn't seem to be any words for it. When he thought about it in English and in song, it was silly, and he felt uncomfortable. Clyde smiled at Wheeler, but Wheeler wasn't paying attention to him now.

Wheeler drove with one hand and with the other he patted Joe Shorty's older son on the head and smiled at Joe Shorty's wife.

"Nice, nice kid," Wheeler said. The woman fidgeted, and she held her other son tightly to her.

Clyde felt her move against him and he tensed. He tried to think of the song then. The People singing, he thought, the woman singing. The mountains, the living, the women strong, the men strong. But he was tense in his mind, and heart. Finally, he said to himself, Okay, potato boss, okay.

They drove into the camp and stopped in front of Clyde's and Willie's shack. Clyde thought, Okay, Potato boss, okay. He opened the door and began to climb out. The woman and her children began to follow him.

"Wait," Wheeler said. "I'll drive you home. I'm going your way." His voice was almost angry.

Wheeler grabbed her arm, but she wrenched away. Clyde stopped and looked at Wheeler.

"She lives over there," Clyde said, pointing to Joe Shorty's shack, but he knew that Wheeler knew that.

Wheeler scowled at him and then he searched for a bottle under the seat. The woman did not move away anymore. She watched Wheeler and then said something to her children. Clyde looked at her. The song, he thought, and he tried very hard to think of the woman singing. The children ran to the shack, and Joe Shorty's woman and Wheeler followed.

For a long time, Clyde stood behind the door of his and Willie's shack. Listening and thinking quiet angry thoughts. He thought of Willie, Joe Shorty, the Elkhorn Bar, Hank Williams, potatoes, the woman and her sons. And he thought of Wheeler and himself, and he asked himself why he was not listening for the song, because he had decided that the woman singing was something a long time ago and would not happen anymore. If it did, he would not believe it. He would not listen. Finally, he moved away from the door and began to search through Willie's things for a bottle. But there was no bottle of anything except the kerosene and for a moment he thought of drinking kerosene. It was a silly thought, and so he laughed.

When the bus pulled out of the town in the morning, Clyde thought of Willie again. Willie had come in when the sun was coming up. He was red-eyed and sick.

"We had a time, son," Willie said. He sat at the table woodenly. He did not notice that Clyde was putting clothes into a grip bag.

"That Wheeler, he sure gets up early. Joe Shorty and I met him outside his house. 'The early bird gets the worms,' he said. Sure funny guy. And he gave us some drinks," Willie mumbled. He was about to fall asleep with his head on the table.

"I'm going home," Clyde said. He had finished putting his clothes in the bag.

"You never have a good time," Willie said. Clyde thought about that and asked in his mind whether that was true or not.

When Clyde thought about the woman's singing he knew that it had been real. Later on he would hear it someplace again and he would believe it. There was a large hurt in his throat and he began to make a song, like those of The People, in his mind.

Where O Where

November, 1974. Poor Billy, I wonder where he went, where he is. I know he doesn't have any money; he never has any money. The only way he can survive is act crazy and stay locked up, play dead, or find someone with sense enough to know he can't take care of himself. I guess I shouldn't but I worry about Billy.

I take a walk and in a while I realize I am looking for Billy Maguirre. I search a crowded stand of cattails and the shadows of trees and the saltcedar groves curving along the river. On the other side of the river are low bluffs of old lava, and there are many crevices. Among the bird shrills and the acres of space between an owl's hollow and deep sounds, where o where is Billy Maguirre. *Fort Lyons VAH.*

Sam thought, I should have gone with Billy Maguirre. He wanted me to go with him.

One day, Billy had said, "Sam, let's take off into the mountains in New Mexico."

Sam didn't pay much attention to him. He said, "Yeah, that's a good idea, Billy."

"I mean it," Billy said. "We'll build us a cabin, not big, just a small cabin with two rooms and a closet to store things in for the winter. And we'll build an outdoors toilet."

Billy was twenty-four but just a kid. He hadn't done very much in his life. He'd gotten drafted into the Army, then got screwed up, maybe dope, wrecked a stolen Army jeep, served time in the stockade. And then he got discharged out of the Army with a medical. And then he didn't do anything, like before, until he was committed into the VAH.

"I had a time," Billy said, talking about the time he didn't do anything, which had been mostly all his life. "We used to ride up in the hills above Blue Valley and hunt rabbits with .22s and cruise our dune-buggies. Sometimes we'd have lots of grass. I used to blow a lot of grass and eat pills. You ever blow lots of grass and eat pills, Sam?"

"No, Billy," Sam would say, "not much."

"I didn't do anything," Billy would say. "That was the life." And then with something serious and quiet in his voice, he'd say, "I want to do something though. I want to travel. See the world, Sam, that's what I want to do." He'd even get a dreamy tone in his voice.

"Yeah," Sam agreed. "See places, meet people, take a ship. Go places you've never been."

"You ever been to Disneyland, Sam?" he asked a couple of times. Sometimes that was the kind of mind Billy had, and Sam thought, Only dumb dreams.

"No, but I've never wanted to go to Disneyland," Sam said the first time. The second time he said, angrily, "Billy, you asked me that stupid question before. Disneyland is a dumb place to go to. Go to the Grand Canyon, Buenos Aires, Montana, the Nile River. Disneyland is a shitty place to go to." He was immediately sorry he said that, because Billy just looked at the ground.

Billy didn't say anything at first and then in a very small voice he said, "I was in Korea. But that was in the Army." He got very quiet then and sad and Sam felt bad for yelling at Billy.

And then lately, Billy got to talking about the mountains in New Mexico and the cabin.

"We can grow things too," he said. "Radishes, I love radishes. And carrots and corn and sweet peas and plant apple trees. I've never planted a tree in my life but hell it shouldn't be that hard." Billy was tickled with himself just thinking about growing apple trees in the mountains.

"That sounds like a lot of work, Billy," Sam said, frowning. He had come to half-seriously go along with Billy's talk about the mountains. "But it'll be good for us," he added. "Exercise and fresh air from morning to night."

That's what Billy needed most, exercise and fresh air, Sam thought. Billy wandered around a lot, looking lost and weary and his skin was the color of old wood lying in a damp corner. He was slouch shouldered and always wore badly fitting clothes but he wasn't a bad-looking kid. But when you saw him shuffling around in the VAH looney you would know right off there was something wrong with him.

"What's the best kind of wood to use for a cabin, Sam? The kind that Indians use?" Bill asked seriously.

Sam was an Indian but he didn't know what kind of wood Indians used for cabins. He didn't know much about being Indian either—he'd grown up in Denver—and he said, "Probably pine, Billy. Yeah I think pine will be okay. Maybe juniper."

Actually, Sam liked talking about the cabin and the mountains. One summer after the Army he tried living by himself in a tipi in southwestern Colorado. Just him and his dog. The next summer he was going to get some land and build a shack on it, nothing fancy he dreamed just a one room shack.

"We better make sure there's water near the cabin," Billy said.

"For sure," Sam said. Near that summer tipi was a small stream, La Plata Creek, that ran from the mountains nearby. It had the coldest and clearest water Sam could remember from anywhere.

And then just the other day, something blew in Billy's head. One of the other patients came running to tell Sam.

The television was on in the Rec Room. The guys were watching Bonanza, and a commercial came on. The commercial was a pretty woman demonstrating which kind of washing soap was the best for grimy clothes. Without any kind of warning, Billy stood up and threw a cue ball from the pooltable through the TV screen. He started yelling and throwing a finger at the broken TV and if someone hadn't grabbed him he would have put his fist through the tube.

Sam watched the aides come and shackle Billy into a leather harness, smoothly shoot him with a syringe of something, and take him down the steps. Sam didn't say anything, and then he turned to stare far away to the bluffs beyond the Arkansas River, beyond the steel-meshed windows.

The next morning when Sam saw Billy stumbling dumbly to the messhall in line with the rest of the zombies from Lock Ward, he thought of what Billy had said months before.

"My old man was really great, Sam. He used to take me and my brother and my little sister to the drive-in rootbeer place in Grayson. He'd buy us rootbeer floats. I loved rootbeer floats. He helped me make an aquarium for a science class in the third grade. I didn't like science in high school but I really liked making that aquarium.

"He worked in the mines, Sam, that's hard work. Shitty work for this company; sometimes he would have to work two shifts, but one day he came home early. My mom wasn't home. She was out shopping at a sale. Three times a week, she would shop at sales. My old man went to find her. A couple hours later, they came home. My mother was crying and she looked real bad in the face. I don't know what happened. Or maybe I did. My old man didn't say much of anything.

"The next day he moved to Utah. I haven't seen him but two short times since then," Billy said.

Sam remembered watching Billy pace back and forth whenever a commercial with a woman came on TV. It didn't matter what the woman was doing, whether it was talking about detergent or a compact car or was teasing up to some guy with a special kind of shaving lotion.

What seemed to matter was that the woman was very pretty and had this very put on smile. That's what made the difference. Billy would get all tensed up and his mouth and face would grimace and Sam would see Billy's adams apple bob up and down in tight swallows. A couple of times Billy had yelled but that was all.

Coming back from messhall at supper, one of the guys said, "Billy Maguirre took off."

Sam wondered, Where the hell could Billy go? He really had no place to go. He has no money. He can't even take care of himself.

A couple of days before, Billy had asked where the nearest mountains were.

They were sitting on the grass in front of Unit 8. Sam pointed beyond the hospital, beyond the dike which held back the Arkansas River when it flooded. "I was looking at the map the other day," he said, "trying to see where the river starts. It starts in the Sawatch Range of the Rocky Mountains. That means if you follow the Arkansas River upstream you'll get to the mountains. It will take about six days, Billy."

Sam followed the river they could not see with his finger westward towards the mountains. "Sawatch," Billy said, "That's an Indian name isn't it, Sam?"

Sam watched Billy repeating the name silently. He started to say, I don't know, and then said, "Yes, it is, Billy."

Billy Maguirre's been gone for a half a day now and it'll be dark soon, Sam thought. He looked towards the river and tried to see it beyond the dike.

You Were Real,
The White Radical Said To Me

I was about to fall on my tired ass, geesus.

Ah man, I get caught into these things. "I'm looking for historical Indians," a woman said on the phone, calling me from a local radio station.

We need an Indian to be an Indian on our Frontiers Day float, another woman had said when I was in the veterans hospital in Colorado.

"Well," this one from the radio station said, "there are Indians and there are Indians, but we need an Indian poet, and you're an Indian poet."

Ah man, and so sometimes I say, Yeah. And then I almost fall on my ass.

The California freeway traffic is always incredible. Incredible but real, so you have to believe it. At night, car and truck lights coming madly at you, passing you by, wheels in front of you wavering, the railing next to you too damn close.

I was supposed to be at Glide Church in San Francisco to read some poems at 9 o'clock or so. It would have to be "or so."

In San Jose it was good to be at the parent and teacher gathering. Indian parents and their children. The white teachers and the school district superintendent looking remote, out of bureaucratic necessity perhaps. Hello, I'm pleased to meet you. They look too bored to be that pleased.

The parents had prepared food, some stew, fry bread, salad and cake. I joked with a Tlingit girl who had sung a Buffy St. Marie song. "You have to cook mutton for ten hours like the Pueblos do for it to be really good—and put chili in it." Laughing.

A Choctaw man smiled and smiled when I told the stories.

"The stories belong to you. Remember that they come from the source of a community: people and people, people and all life. These songs and the words of them come from the nature of all life. The stories come from the source and nature of all life. Remember that," I told the parents, their children, the teachers and the superintendent who still looked bored. "You are part of them."

I watched a Pueblo woman sitting at the school cafeteria table with her two children. "I learned this song by listening to some thoughts about a horse found high up in the Andes Mountains. The bones were twelve thousand years old." The woman's daughters were about eight and ten years old.

We swung off the freeway into the city and into the Fillmore and into the Tenderloin.

"Magic," I said, "we need magic to find a parking space." We found one in the church parking lot. All the spaces had signs: Reserved. But tonight, all the spaces in the church are not filled, so we park.

We trudged up some creaking stairs in what looked, at first, like a deserted building. The white organizers sat at a rickety table upstairs with posters, leaflets, newsletters, buttons, cans for money. They looked sort of bored too.

There were a few Indians at the benefit fund-raiser. We met Paul leaving. Hey man, I need an Apache to talk with, tell me about the mountains at home. But he was in a hurry. I have to go, brother, have to go over to the St. Francis. And he clumped on down the stairs with a pretty woman on his arm.

Geesus, sometimes, I don't know why I say I will do it. This place is a church, and I know churches are places where you are to bring your tired bones and shredded soul for salvation but, man, I don't know why I say, Yes, sometimes.

There seemed to be a large crowd but as we sat down some people were leaving. It had been a long day and a long frenetic drive from San Jose, and I was tired, and I know that I feel sorry, perhaps unreasonably, for myself sometimes.

Several Chippewa men from Minnesota sang around the AIM drum and one of their leaders spoke eloquently and strongly. We are all Indians. After he spoke, a couple of young radical whites approached the microphone and haggled with each other until one won over the other. "We need money. We have many expenses to meet. Give what you can," he said. Coffee cans were passed through the crowd.

I wondered how Sid was doing in Indio county jail in southern California. I wondered how Crow Dog was doing in Lewisburg prison.

Kuntsler, the daddy lawyer of the radicals, perched his glasses at the top slope of his forehead and spoke. "There is a revolution going on in America. There is a change going on." He got several spates of applause. Several times he pushed his glasses securely to the apex of his forehead.

There was an Indian that I caught sitting at a corner of my eyesight. The red coals of his eyes were smoldering. He tottered from the welling in his stomach.

Several Chicano women and men in their twenties and thirties got on stage. They sang rousing songs for the spirited and rising and united forces of the people. We shall come alive. We are all Indians. The words and the music vibrated among those who were left. Even the tense and tired muscles of my body became rhythms.

So it was finally my turn. I thought I was almost ready to leave but I stayed. I always stay. Even if I am ready to fall on my ass, even if I feel unreasonably sorry for myself sometimes. So I stumbled up the steps to the stage.

Ah man, I say I don't know why I do it but I do. I do it for myself, for my people, for the source, for the words that are sacred because they come from a community of people and all life. And I do it because I ache for help, because we all need help. And that's the way I read the poems that night.

The words come from the old man, Clay, who carried a brown leather bag on his shoulder as he moved among our people, teaching them. They come from the Felipe brothers who led a New Mexico state cop unto Acoma land and then wiped him out. They come from the brown man with stifled and troubled dreams sprawled at the corner of 5th and Mission. They come from the dread and unfortunate Arizona winter of Beauty Roanhorse somewhere between Klagetoh and Sanders Bar. Ah man, they come from me, they come from them, and I return those words.

The smoldering in the eyes of that Indian man almost caught full fire.

Feeling Old

Nome was eighty-one years old now, and he felt old. *Felt* old—he hadn't before, had always felt young, at least in his mind if not in body. Of course he did—he'd often thought to himself—even mornings just out of bed, when suddenly, in his seventies, it seemed the muscle all went out of him. And he'd just sit in a chair or on the edge of his bed, and he would even get up painfully and pull the curtains together on his window and stay very still in the gray light. But he would always get up after several moments and jerk open the curtains and raise the window to breathe the air from the outside. He'd always done that, never let his spirit flag, but that was then. Then. And then during his seventy-ninth year, sometime during, he couldn't tell when it was—it must have happened gradually, subtly—his emotions got tired. It may have been like the redness in his eyes turning to an ache and he couldn't tell when the moment was that the dull ache began. He just noticed that it was there—the tiredness of his emotion happened like that. He noticed then it was there.

Nome thought he could remember or perhaps it was that he was trying hard to reconstruct the moment. He'd gotten up that morning, brushed the teeth he still had, felt his beard with the tips of his fingers, washed, and then went to the kitchen to put on some coffee. A couple or several years before, a doctor had told him to cut back on coffee, but he hadn't managed to, and he hadn't wanted to. He had said to himself that he'd always enjoyed the morning smell of coffee, and it made him recall years back when he'd rise to go to work at the lumber yard where he'd been foreman, when the spring mornings were fresh and good. Coffee smell was a special tinge to the fresh and good. Then. But it had happened, right after he had finished scrambling eggs in his favorite wood handled pan. He noticed that the eggs were curdled into a yellow-gray mess. He had put the raisin bread on for toast, and they had popped out of the toaster. He looked at the brown bread momentarily, and then he turned his head back to the eggs. He didn't know, suddenly and uncertainly, if he was hungry or not. Some mornings he wasn't hungry and other mornings he was ravenous, but he always knew one way or the other. This morning he didn't know. And there were the curdled eggs getting dry and the toast getting cold and the coffee had stopped perking. So he sat down at the kitchen table. He felt that tiredness then, and it was in the body and spirit and his emotion.

Now, it was the middle of the morning as he recalled that reconstruction. Then he had gotten himself eventually out of his tiredness and uncertainty and he worked in his garden; it had been early spring and he wanted to ready the ground for planting at the end of the month. He could do that then, working himself away and out of it. Then. But now he was eighty-one years old.

Alma, his granddaughter, had come to see him a couple of weeks before. She'd driven in her VW from Baton Rouge where she went to college, and he'd heard her funny car beep when she drove up to the front yard. He didn't get off the couch he was lying on with the unfolded newspaper lying loose in his hand. She'd knocked, and knocked again, and he could hear her call. Finally, he got up, put on his slippers and went to the door. Grand Nome, Grand Nome, Alma said, hollering actually. And he let her hug him. Nome, I decided to come stay with you for a day since you're my favorite fella, she said, and he had managed to smile. She looked around the room and announced, I see you haven't been following your rule. He must have looked perplexed, and she explained. Tidiness and orderliness, Alma said. It was a reference to the years before when he had advised his grandchildren about the conduct of life, how order and neatness were always helpful. Alma started with the dishes and moved into the living room by midafternoon, putting the unfolded newpapers into a pile, straightening things, and then vacuuming. All of the while, she kept up an enthusiastic chatter. She talked about chemistry, philosophy, and values. Her peers at college didn't seem to know or didn't want to know about hard work and struggle and sharing she said, and she told him that she had spoken about him during a political science class.

I told them, Alma said, that my Grand Nome was a working man from the word go and he—you!—always spoke for the struggle of the common man. I told them about your years as a merchant seaman and then the lumber yard. They were really interested and then the instructor asked me if you'd come up to the college to talk. Would you, Grand Nome? Would you? Nome didn't know one way or the other. He didn't know, so in order to seem decisive he eventually said, No. No. It'll be fun, Nome, come on. You can ride back with me. I've got an apartment, Alma said, you can sleep in my bed and I'll sleep in my bedroll. But he didn't know and it bothered him that it was a feeling like he didn't know whether he was hungry or not, so he said, No. He didn't want her to know that he didn't know or didn't care if he did one way or the other. He said, I'm fixing my garden soil for planting later this month. He said that although he didn't know whether or not he would ever plant again. When Alma was ready to leave the next day, she asked one more time, and Nome didn't say anything then; he just sat at the kitchen table and shook his head with a vague smile and then let her hug him goodbye.

A week later, he was tired and old. Dierdra, his other granddaughter called him on the telephone in the afternoon. She said, Grandpa, Alma told me she'd visited and stayed with you, and I thought I'd call. Yes, she did, Nome said, it was nice of Alma to visit me. But he didn't feel any certain way about it. It was insincere what he said but he said it—It was nice of her. How are you, Grandpa? Dierdra asked. I'm fine, dear, he said, just fine. But he was tired and old. And when they finished talking, he felt the entire weight of his tiredness and age upon him. He knew that his granddaughters meant well and he could appreciate that, but he didn't think any certain way about it; it didn't seem to make any difference. Now, the vague light in the room with the curtains drawn on the windows felt like it had the same weight as his tiredness and heavy age.

Anything

He told that young vet, "Anything," when the vet asked him what he wrote. That wasn't true. He thought, Anything is damn hard to write; that is, anything that is something.

Once, he wrote a story about a dog named Old Horse. He had just come home from a trip to the East, and he was tired. He came in at midnight or so from the airport, a bar or two on the way home. His wife was not very happy.

She went back to bed as soon as she saw it was him fumbling to lock the door.

The next morning she said, "There is nothing I can do about you."

As usual he didn't eat any breakfast, just black coffee, and he was talking with their son. The boy was three years old, and he had shaken his father awake earlier. He had awoken but his head was spinning, and he knew he was breaking his own heart again.

"What do you mean?" he said, lamely, knowing exactly what she meant, of course.

"This," she said, her voice an even tone, merely stating facts. "You're away so much of the time and when you come home you're all messed up again. I mean it. There is nothing nobody can do about you. I want you to leave."

Okay, he said to himself. And to her, but he didn't want her to know, so he didn't say anything or look at her. So I'll leave. I don't know where the hell I'll go. Probably sleep on the floor of the office that's where.

He had slept there before. It was certainly no home away from home, in fact it was a crummy place to sleep, right on the main drag of the city, traffic and sirens all night long, the backdoor night light of the drugstore next door glaring through the windows. The shadows of the window frames falling on to the hard tile floor.

50

That morning he didn't feel like going to work.

She went to class. She was a student at the University. She took their son to the babysitter's. When they left, he was in the bathroom taking a shower. He took deep breaths and scrubbed and scrubbed, but he could not get rid of his exhaustion and hangover.

Pouring the rest of the morning coffee, he got this feeling as he watched a mongrel dog crossing the street. The dog was a skinny cur, grayish, a nothing mutt. He felt like the dog. He got this missing feeling for the dog he had when he was a boy. The dog's name was Bony. It was his brother's and his. The dog had gotten run over by a damn diesel truck. They buried Bony by the side of U.S. 66.

He sat down and took a notepad from his back pocket. He used to carry them all the time, all dogeared and worn. He would jot down scribbles which were many times undecipherable, and he wrote down any sort of thing in them. This time he wrote about Old Horse, a dog he remembered from that feeling he had.

It was from a long time before, but that morning, hungover, feeling the way he did, wretched and alone, made it easy enough. But he wrote only a sentence or two before he looked out the window again and thought he might have enough change for a jug of something. He searched through his pockets, and it was there, something for the morning. And he walked up to the grocery mart and got something to make the story come easier.

The story wasn't easier. Now as he thought about the young vet asking him the question, he thought, That's a lie. It's easy to think it comes easier, but it doesn't. Nobody can tell me it does. I would tell them they're full of crap. You just put it off with some sort of excuse that's all and you get nothing done.

He thought, That's what I should have told that vet who was impressed I was a writer or trying to be, standing there in front of my typewriter here in the VA hospital, waiting for me to write something. I should have said, "You can write anything but it's got to be something too." But I didn't.

He had written that story about Old Horse and two boys growing up and later it was published. But it wasn't easy writing anything. Especially on mornings like that when his wife had just told him there was nothing anyone—except himself—could do and he had better leave. Nothing. And he had answered, Okay, but he didn't know where the hell he was going to go.

Loose

Loose. That's what he said. Nothing else but that. And he repeated it. Loose.

I'd asked him his name.

I was sitting in the cafe on Central, nursing a coffee. The coffee had gone cold. And he had walked in. Maybe thirty years old, maybe twenty-five.

Brown, scarred face, black hair a mess and long. No grin on his face then. But a smirk that was not intentional it seemed. Shiny eyes tending towards flat.

That's the way I've been, he said. Years and years. Loose.

He just walked on up, maybe he recognized me. I don't know—or thought he did. The table was kind of wobbly and when he pulled a chair to it and leaned on the table, it almost toppled over. But he didn't notice. And he looked at me. Maybe he thought he knew me.

Hi, I said, not loud. Just Hi—like I was looking into a mirror and saying it.

He didn't say anything. I grinned foolishly, not knowing what to do next. And then I told him my name.

So what—the look on his face said. So I'm Indian too, I almost said it out loud. I thought of offering to buy him a coffee. But he would be indifferent to it. He was loose.

So we just sat there.

I didn't like what I'd thought about the mirror. So I asked, Where you from?

Denver, last time, he said, but nowhere really. Here for now.

Brown and scarred, he was looking at me. Studying me, like I was studying him. I should have expected that's what he would say. Nowhere.

Going nowhere. Coming from nowhere. It's scary to think about it. I mean I know what that means. No wonder I'd thought about the mirror.

I've been to Denver, I said. Are you from the north?

He looked away from me.

North, south, east, up, down—what difference does it make, he said. Does it to you?

Sometimes. Most times, I said to convince myself.

He stared hard at me with his almost-flat eyes. His voice could have been a club. Tell me then—what the hell difference does it make?

A tension had gathered in my neck muscles. I thought a moment, looked down at my cold coffee, and then shook my head.

I don't know for sure, I said, but it makes a difference. It's not a philosophical question. . .

Shit, he said, a goddamn intellectual Indian. What the hell is this. Philsophy. You don't know. You're just another dumb Indian. You don't know.

Alright. I didn't know what to say. But it makes a difference. This was a cafe, it was nighttime, the city's main street was busy with traffic, we were sitting here. We'd come from someplace. And we were going someplace.

I'm from here, I said, in New Mexico. I grew up west of here. I've been other places but this is where I'm from.

He didn't look at me. He was looking at the counter where orders for food and drinks were placed. But his face showed nothing—nothing.

I was born in this town even, at the Indian hospital. When people ask me where I'm from I tell them I'm from here.

He still didn't say a word. Alright, Loose, I thought. You've seen the scars on my own face.

See that girl, he said.

I looked. She was behind the counter. She had a paper cap on her head, and she was busy with coffee, taking orders, punching the cash register.

Yeah, I said. The girl was ordinary, kind of cute. Yeah, I said again.

She looks like someone from Alberta.

So he was from the north. Cree, Chippewa probably. He had big hands but he wasn't tall. His hands looked like they'd handled a lot of shit work. Timber, roughnecking. Brutal work.

You want coffee? I asked. There was change on the table.

He looked at me, then at the change. He picked it up and walked over to the counter.

I watched him wait for her to notice him. The muscles at the side of his face moved, like in a grin. The girl looked at him blankly and took his order. And when she turned to get the coffee from the hot plate, he watched her back.

She put the coffee in front of him and I saw her lips move. Asking for the money. He said something again. And her face was startled, embarassed, and then it froze up. And she punched the cash register. He turned and walked back to the table. He spilled some of his coffee.

She sort of looks like someone from Alberta—but not much, he said. And then he grinned wrly. And I had to grin too.

In the newspaper supplement recently I read a small item. It was about children in Ecuador who made a makeshift life on the streets of Quito. Running numbers, stealing from tourists. Prostitutes and fools. The supplement article said they were a dangerous element—like a bomb—in modern Ecuadoran society. Many of them were orphans. They came to the city because it gathered their energy and gave them a mission.

I wanted to tell Loose those street kids had the courage to survive. And more than that—the courage would be the redemption of their lives and Ecuador.

He finished his coffee and stood up.

I didn't ask him where he was going. Okay, I thought.

Loose, he said. Stay loose.

Okay, I said. You too.

With a foolish sort of grin, he walked away, out the door, and up the street.

More Than Anything Else
in the World

It did matter. It mattered more than anything else in the world.

In San Diego, several days before he had been walking in the evening along the beach. A dog ran up to him and sniffed his knees and his pants cuffs. "Hello, puppy," he said. The dog, a German shepherd, looked up at his face, wagged its tail, and then bounded off to join a couple who waved at him.

There were lights out some distance from the shore. It was a boat or an off-shore drilling rig. The lights bobbed up and down. The horizon was metal and dark clouds. It was sometime past sunset.

He knew that California was not for him. He knew that he could live there but it was almost impossible for him. He had known that for a long time, but there were things he always denied so strongly, the things he knew.

So he had boarded the eastbound bus the day before. Early, early in the morning he sat in the Phoenix bus depot. He tried to read a book of contemporary American short stories. There was not a single story in the paperback which rang familiar to him. The sentences and words were just sentences and words.

The sun was rising as the bus pulled into the parking lot of Howard Johnson's in Gallup, New Mexico. Pulling his denim jacket snugly to him to ward away the cold March wind, he got out of the bus. He shivered. The sun rose a weak orange against a heavy gray sky.

On the bus out of Phoenix, he had talked with a woman who sat in the empty seat beside him. He had told her about the dog on the beach in San Diego. The woman was a French tutor in Albuquerque. At the Howard Johnson's breakfast stop, they found a table and continued their conversation.

"Ritual is important for me," he said. "I try to do certain things in the morning, hopefully not only methodically but meaningfully. I try to make them work meaningfully in the ordinary scheme of things, making them an important part of what I do everyday."

"My grandmother went to Mass every morning," the French tutor said. "That was her ritual. I don't think I do very much ritual. I brush my teeth, go to the toilet, comb my hair, fix toast and coffee. The usual things; they don't seem very important."

They ordered eggs, toast, coffee. He watched a woman with long and dark hair sitting a couple of tables away. She wore a red dress with a necklace of shell which brought out the red vividly. He remembered his wife talking about a red dress.

He thought and then he said, "I pray. Mostly, I pray. It can be done anytime, anyplace. I need to." He remembered the desperate prayers on some mornings. He remembered the taut nerves tearing at the precarious mornings. He remembered the feathers clogged in his throat on those mornings. Sometimes it had nothing to do with ritual; prayer was simple necessity.

When the passengers finished their breakfasts, the bus loaded up again. It was the last stretch of the highway for him. And then he would be back where he had begun. California was already a memory. He looked out the bus window.

As the bus drew up to the bus depot, an Indian woman was crossing the Gallup city street. Several men followed her as she walked around to the side of a nearby building. She clutched a bottle in a paper bag under her arm. She wore a sateen green blouse and a long skirt. The woman looked old, and the weary lines in her face made her sadness and her oldness sag.

The men gathered around her as she opened the paper bag. From the bus, several people watched curiously the ritual of the Indians. As he slouched down into his seat, watching out of the corners of his eyes, he heard some of the passengers snicker.

It did matter. He had watched himself in the mirror of his memory. It was another person he saw but it looked so much like himself that he could almost not bare to remember. He had searched every aspect of the image and found himself looking frightened out of yellowed eyes.

"Of course, I realize it is important," the French tutor said. "I believe that the learning process of a child is tied in completely with how the culture that he grows up in functions. A child cannot learn important values unless his culture lets him."

That wasn't what he meant. He had meant the Indian woman and the men sucking at the wine bottle against the wall of the Gallup bus depot. He had meant the escape from southern California. He had said, "Human beings learn from the pressures that are exerted upon them. One's strength buckling under sometimes, that's the main learning process."

The sun was rising into the mid-morning sky. They would soon be near his home where he had been a child. He closed his eyes and tried to sleep. The French tutor dozed off and she leaned into him.

She smelled slightly sweaty and perfumed with some sweet scent. He tried to push her away without disturbing her but she opened her eyes slightly, looked at him, smiled, and leaned closer into him. She was very warm.

The bus passed by his home land. He wanted to wake her up and explain to her. But she was sound asleep and he didn't wake her. He looked and looked to the south where his childhood home was. He looked and looked for a boy walking toward the garden and field that would soon be planted with spring seed.

When the woman awoke, she sighed and snuggled into him. She opened her sleepy eyes and then she reached her far hand to him and put her fingers around his hand. She held him very gently and securely. "I had a dream," she said. "It was so warm and so . . . so comfortable."

He had been dozing a little and he looked at her. He put his other hand over hers. He felt her movement toward him.

"Do you mind?" she asked. She squeezed his hand.

"No," he said, shaking his head.

When the bus pulled into the depot in Albuquerque, she said, "Come with me." She said it firmly, and repeated, "Come with me."

"No," he said. He knew his wife didn't know that he was coming home. He knew that his wife didn't want him home. But he said, "No." It mattered more than anything else in the world that he say, "No."

The Way You See Horses

The boy and his father had taken two willow sticks and carefully split them. The willow was dry and very light but not very strong. The boy's father took his pocket knife, tested the blade's sharpness with his thumb and split the sticks in half.

"I think they'll do," the father said.

"I hope they don't break," the boy said. He held one of the sticks in his hand. It was so light he could barely feel its weight. He felt its tension as he bent it into a slight arc.

"Be careful you don't bend it too far," his father said. He notched the other stick a half inch from each end. That was for the string.

They had gotten a plastic bag from under the kitchen sink that morning. It was a heavy duty bag, the kind that TV advertisements say won't break even if a car engine is put in it. And some tape to hold the plastic bag ends.

"Now," the father said, "we have the sticks, string, plastic bag, and all we need is a tail. And we'll put it all together."

"What's the tail for, Dad?" the boy asked. He had seen tails on kites before but he didn't know what they were for.

"It's to keep one end, the bottom of the kite, weighed down and upright. So it'll fly right," the father explained.

As they were putting the kite upon the sticks and tying its string, the wind picked up some. It gusted with sudden quick movements. It billowed out the plastic bag so that the father had to hold one end of the bag down with his knee while he trimmed one end and began to fit it to the crossed form of willow sticks.

After several moments, the wind died down quietly and they soon finished the kite.

"Now we need a tail don't we, Dad?" the boy said.

"Yeah. Let's see what we can use," the father said. He picked up a strip of the plastic bag but it seemed too light and he looked around some more. They were at the edge of a park and there didn't seem to be much of anything around.

He searched in his pockets and he found a red flowered handkerchief. He bit at an edge of the handkerchief and tore a narrow strip off. He cut several more strips until there wasn't anything of the handkerchief left.

His son watched him very closely.

"That's okay," his father said, "I've got another booger rag just like the other one." He smiled and ruffled the boy's hair.

"Booger rag," the boy said and he giggled and squealed with laughter. "Booger rag."

The boy's father knotted the strips together and then he cut a bit of the string and tied the tail to the bottom of the kite.

"Now let's see what we have here?" the father said grandly. "Why it's the genuine article, a real handmade kite. Here, Inspector, you want to pass inspection on it?" He handed the fragile-looking plastic bag and willow stick kite to the boy.

The boy held it in his hands and looked it over. It flapped some in a gust of wind. It felt almost alive and he was smiling as his father tied the end of the ball of string to the sticks.

"Now, you walk out a ways over that way," the father said. He pointed to the northeast in the direction the wind was blowing.

"Just a minute, son. Let's wait a bit until the wind goes down just a bit," the father said. "Otherwise, it might tear loose on us." They waited for several moments.

"Okay. Okay, now. Hold it up," he told his son as the wind quieted down to a gentler pace, "and then let it go." He held the ball of string. "Now. Let it go."

The boy let the kite go. It wobbled and kicked in the wind at the end of the string. His father fed out the string from the ball as he walked slowly in the direction the kite was flying. Soon, it was flying pretty high.

"Here, now you hold it for a while. Keep the string taut some and give it more string," the father said. He held out the ball of string to his son.

The boy took it. The string vibrated in his hand and fingers. It was like it was really alive. He could feel the kite jump and kick and tremble at the end of the string. The wind was powerful. The kite swung and made half loops and sudden arcs. The sky was mostly blue but there was a small mass of white clouds towards which the kite climbed.

"A bit taut now, son," the father said. "Walk back a little." They had moved yards away from where they had let the kite go. He watched his son watching the string inch from his hand and then turn his head to the tumbling and gliding kite. He suddenly felt the aching and desperate loneliness he often felt when he would be alone someplace and he would wish he could be with his young son at that very moment.

The boy was intense with the kite. The kite jerked and then steadied and balanced perfectly in the sky and stopped dead still for just an instant and then jumped alive again.

The kite was at the edge of the outline of white clouds.

"Dad, the kite is going to hit the clouds," the boy hollered.

The boy's sudden voice startled his father and they locked glances for the briefest moment. The kite string was a thin almost invisible line in the sky but it was there and it was kicking alive and vibrating in the boy's hand. The father looked at the kite and the clouds.

"No, it won't," he said. "The clouds are quite high. They're way over there." He pointed to some hills in the east.

The boy pulled back on the string anyway and he walked backwards a few steps. The kite looped and tumbled as it seemed to bump upon the clouds. The wind was quieter where he stood. The string trembled.

"The clouds don't look far away," the boy said after a while, "but they are." And he continued, "When you look at the kite and it's reflected against the clouds, it makes the clouds look like they're close. But they're not. It's the way they look to you."

The father looked at the clouds again and at the kite. He watched the string vibrating in his son's hand. He looked at his son. His son's eyes were lit with the depth of the blue sky and his boyhood.

Yes, of course, the father thought, that's the reason why the clouds look like they're so close. So close you could touch them. It's the way you see them.

There were horses in the sky. They moiled and tumbled into the shapes of their motion. They were playing. They were young colts and mares and old studs. They thundered silently across the flat broad plain of the blue sky. The horses were flying. They were trembling in the string that the boy held in his hands. The boy could feel the bones, the eyes, the rippling muscle and skin, the power and the motion of the horses.

The father said, "The clouds are like horses. You can imagine horses in them. Can you see them?"

His son watched the clouds for several moments and then he said, "Yeah. Yeah, Dad, I can see them. They're almost for real horses. It's the same way that the clouds seem to be real close, like my kite is touching them. It's the way you see them."

"Yeah," his father said. It's the way you see them.

The Panther Waits

"That people will continue longest in the enjoyment of peace who timely prepare to vindicate themselves and manifest a determination to protect themselves whenever they are wronged." Tecumseh, 1811

Tahlequah is cold in November, and Sam, Billy and Jay sat underneath a lustreless sun. They had been drinking all afternoon. Beer. Wine. They were talking, trying not to feel the cold.

Maybe we need another vision, Billy.

Ah shoot, vision. I had one last night and it was pretty awful—got run over by a train and somebody stole my wife.

He he he. Have another beer, Billy.

Maybe though, you know. It might work.

Forget it, huh. Cold beer vision, that's what I like.

No, Sam, I mean I've been thinking about that old man that used to be drunk all the time.

Your old man, he he he, he was drunk all the time.

Yeah, but not him. He was just a plain old drunk. I mean Harry Brown, that guy that sat out by the courthouse a lot. He used to have this paper with him.

Harry J. Brown you mean? He was a kook, a real kookie kook, that one?

Yeah. Well, one time me and my brother, Taft, before he died in that car wreck down by Sulphur, well me and him we asked Harry to buy us some beer at Sophie's Grill, you know, and he did. And then he wanted a can and sure we said but we had to go down by the bridge before we would give him one. We did and sat down by the bushes there and gave him a beer.

Yeah, we used to too. He'd do anything for a beer, old Harry J. Brown. And your brother, he was a hell of a drinker too, he he he.

We sat and drank beer for a while, just sitting, talking a bit about fishing or something, getting up once in a while to pee, and just bullshitting around. And then we finished all the beer and was wishing we had more but we had no money, and we said to Harry, Harry, we gotta go now.

He was kind of fallen asleep, you know, just laid his head on his shoulder like he did sometimes on the cement courthouse steps. We shook his shoulder.

Uh, uh yeah, he said. And then he sort of shook his head and sort of like cleared his eyes with his hand, you know, like he was seeing kind of far and almost like we were strangers to him, like he didn't know us although we'd been together all afternoon.

We said we was leaving, and he looked straight up into Taft's eyes and then over to me and then back to Taft. And then he rubbed his old brown hand over his eyes again and said, Get this. He said, Yes, kinda slow in his voice and careful, Yes, it's true and it will come true.

I just realized, Harry Brown said slowly but clearly then, not like later on when you'd hardly understand what he was saying at the courthouse.

Realized, he repeated, you're the two. Looking straight into Taft's and my eyes. And then he kind of smiled and made a small laugh and then he shook and started to cry.

Harry, Taft said, you old fool, what the hell you talking about. C'mon, get a hold of yourself, shape up, old buddy. Taft always liked to talk to old guys. Sometimes nobody else would talk to them or make fun of them—remember? But Taft was always buddies with them.

Yeah, they gave him wine, that wino, Sam giggled. He knew how to hit them up.

Anyway, Harry sat up then and didn't look at us no more but he said, Sit down, I want to show you something. And then he pulled out this paper.

It was just a old piece of paper, sort of browned and folded, soft looking like he'd carried it a long time. Listen, he said and then he didn't say anything. And we said again, We gotta go soon, Harry.

Wait. Wait, he said, you just wait. It's time to be serious and sure.

He said, They travelled all over. They went south, west,

north, east, all those states now that you learn about in books. Even Florida, even Mississippi, even Missouri, all over they did.

Who did? Taft asked. I was wondering myself.

The two brothers. Look, you can see their marks and their roads. He was pointing with his shaky old scarred finger. That old man had thick fingers. I've seen him lift a beer cap off the old kind of beer bottle with his thumb. The scar was from when the state police slammed his hand some years ago.

Taft was looking at the paper with a curious look on his face. I mean curious and serious too. I still couldn't see anything. Nothing. I thought maybe there was a faint picture of something but there didn't seem to be anything—just paper.

Taft looked over at me then and made a motion with his chin and I looked at the paper again and listened.

They tried to tell all the people. They said, You Indians— they meant all the Indians where ever they went and even us now I'm sure—you Indians must be together and be one people. You are all together on this land. This land is your home and you must see yourself as all together. You people, you gotta understand this. There is no other way we're gonna be able to save our land and our people unless we decide to be all together.

The brothers travelled all over. Alabama, Canada, Kentucky, Georgia, all those states now on the map. Some places people said to them, We don't want to be together. We're always fighting with those other people. They don't like us and we don't like them. They steal and they're not trustworthy.

But the brothers insisted, We are all different people that's for sure, but we are all human people, all humankind, all sisters and brothers, and this is all our land. We have to settle with each other. No more fighting, no more arguing, because it is the land and our home we have to fight for. That is what we have come to convince you about.

The brothers said, We will all have to fight before it's too late. They are coming. They keep coming and they want to take our land and our people. We have told them, No, we cannot sell our mother earth, we cannot sell the ocean, we cannot sell the air, we cannot give our lives away. We will have to defend them and we must do it all together. We must do it, the brothers said. Listen.

Taft just kept looking at the paper and the brown finger of

Harry Brown moving over the paper, and I kept looking too. I still didn't see anything except the wrinkles and fold of the paper but what Harry was saying with his serious story voice put something there I think, and I looked over at Taft again. He was nodding his head like he understood perfectly what the old man was saying.

They were talking about the Americans coming and they wanted the Indians to be all together so they could help each other fight them off. So they could save their land and their families. That's what I remembered just a while ago. I thought I'd forgotten but I don't think I'll ever forget. It's as close to me as you two are.

Harry paused and then he went on. They were two brothers like you are. One of them, the older, was called Tecumtha. I've heard it means the panther in waiting. And the other was one who had old drunk problems like me, but he saved himself and helped his people. Maybe the vision they said he had came from his sickness of drinking, but it happened and they tried to do something about it. That's what is on here, look.

And Taft and I looked again, but I still couldn't see anything. But I didn't say so, and Taft said, Yeah, Harry, I see.

And then we had to go. We was supposed to pick up some bailing wire from Stokes Store and take it back to our old man. Before we left, Harry looked up at us again, straight into our faces. His eyes had cleared you know, and he said, They were two brothers.

Taft and I talked some about it and then later on somebody—you know Ron and Jimmy, the two brothers from up by Pryor?

Yeah, Jimmy the all-state fullback? Boy, was he something. Yeah, I know them.

Yeah. Well, Ron told me old Harry Brown told them that same story too, but they couldn't see nothing on the paper either. They said it was kind of blue not brownish like I'd seen. I told Taft and he said, Well those two guys are too dumb and ignorant to see anything if it was right in front of their nose.

Jimmy got a scholarship to college and works for an oil company down in Houston and Ron, I think, he's at the tribal office, desk job and all that, doing pretty good. I said to Taft, You didn't see anything either. And he looked at me kind of pissed and said, Maybe not but I know what Harry meant.

Geesus, that Taft could drink. He coulda been something too but he sure could drink like a hurricane, he he he. Tell us again what happened, Jay.

No, Sam, it was just a car wreck.

Maybe we need another vision, Billy said.

Hiding, West Of Here

I got to thinking of it all: this mountain has been here for a long, long time, just being here, sitting and growing trees, grass, oak brush; boulders and slab rock slowly sliding down the sides. Funny, I never thought about it before. I mean I come up here a lot, and I've seen it and I've felt it. Usually, I come up that road from Grants into Lobo Canyon, the little creek running beside the road, then up this way. And I drive off the road a ways on a little dirt trail that nobody ever uses much and I sort of hide. Yeah, sort of hide you might call it, my car off into the trees. I guess even thinking that I'd park it so nobody would see it if they'd happen to be passing by on the bigger road. And then I'd come sit on some rocks. Like this one here. Well that's what makes me think about it now, sitting here by the mountain, that peak behind me, rocks around me, because one afternoon I was sitting here, sort of hidden, and, well I'll explain it.

I work on the other side of that long lava mesa at Ambrosia Lake at a mine section there. I come out from home, West Virginia, in 1958, got on at Kerr McGee, then quit and went over to Phillips for a while. And then back to Kerr McGee again until I quit for a while, but I got a trade as a mechanic and the pay's good and I don't have to go underground much anymore so now I'm back with the company again. I had to work shift before but now it's all days, five days a week, kids all grown and out of high school; my youngest daughter is in nursing school now. So I'm doing alright.

But being mechanic at the mines, it's still hard work, cold in winter, hotter'n the dickens in the summer, even underground when ventilation goes out and you have to go down, get it back in operation, that's the shits. And new guys coming in all the time, you can't depend on them; some bums come to work shaky and badminded, give everyone trouble, can't trust them with tools and equipment. Accidents. I've seen some bad ones, company's fault most of them but it don't ever look that way; superintendent, company rules, regulations set up that way— man can't do anything to make him feel ahead.

I've worked hard all my life. My daddy was a coalminer, grandpa too, and it's work that's hard, and sometimes you feel good, strong, but it's shitwork too so you feel there's no profit in being a man. So I come sometimes on Sundays, come up here, and well, yeah, hide out. It's my time, the mountain at my back, over my shoulder, and I can't hear anything except the wind brushing through the trees and laying unto the cliffs, these here, at my feet. It's my time and the mountain's time.

One afternoon I was here just kind of listening, watching sparrows or some kind of bird a while, and then I heard some breathing hard. I mean, man kind of breathing, heavy and low on breath, like some fellow down in the mine shoveling rock ore or drilling and I used to wonder why anybody would torture themselves like that but they got to make a living. Well, I heard that breathing and I looked around but I couldn't see anything, and then I figured it to be coming from below. And I looked down there past the cliff edge and I seen these Indians. Two of them.

They were coming out of the trees, pines, coming towards the bottom of the cliff, and they were puffing away, the old man mostly. He was pretty old, maybe eighty, and the younger man about fifty who looked older actually than he was due to a heavy gut and a tired face. Sweat was pouring off him, and the old man was actually in pretty good shape but for his breathing like I've known guys at home with the black lung; they can't breathe and they can't climb mountains. Not like this old guy. Well, those Indians, they were up to something I could tell that. They were dressed in blankets; I mean blankets were wrapped around their hips and shoulders and they had beads around their necks and a little pouch at their sides. I seen pictures of Indians about like that.

I've worked with several, younger fellows, 'bout twenty and thirty years old, and one of the younger ones once I asked him why he wore this little bag on his leather belt; he was the only one who did. We were eating lunch, and he looked up at me, and he drank some coffee from his thermos cup and then he said, You know that stope we was working this morning? And I said,

Yeah. Well, he said, you know that ain't very well shored and you notice some bolts cracking loose. I'd noticed them and I said, Yeah. Well, he patted his pouch, this keeps it from falling down on us 'cause the damn company don't. He said this I noticed seriously though maybe with a kind of bullshit drama too. There was another Indian fellow eating with us and I looked over at him and then this one looked up from his lunchpail and grinned and said, That stuff he keeps in that little bag keeps him up too. And he pinched up his fingers to his mouth like it was a roll-your-own he was holding and sucked at it and grinned and laughed. So I grinned too.

Well, they were young fellows. I got along with them. One of them talked about what the mining companies were doing to the land; that was the younger one. He'd go on about whites and America and destruction; shit, shit, like that. Which I go along with sometimes but other times I don't. I worked with them and knew they were no different from myself and other workers who have to make a living at that kind of work.

But this time, that afternoon, when I was hiding, sitting on a rock by the cliff edge, I wasn't expecting anything. Just sitting there, kind of thinking, the blue sky far out there, the wind cutting through the trees, silence. And then along with the breathing there was a kind of clacking noise too, like shells rattling together. I looked at what the two Indians were doing. They had taken their blankets off and rolled them up and laid them aside on a rock. And then they took some things out of a bundle which they had strapped across each of their backs. I didn't know whether to keep watching or what. It was private, see—and I could see they were looking around like they might be checking to see if someone might be watching and when the younger man turned his head towards me, I ducked my head below his line of sight. I thought about my watching and later I looked again; I never seen anything like that.

My wife and I, and the kids when they were still home, shop in Grants and we see a lot of Indians. Just shopping, weekends, Christmas, and they'd be buying the usual things. Lots of flour though, like folks who make their own bread, folks in West Virginia when I was a kid did that. Lots of kids usually sitting in the back of trucks out in the parking lot, some of them not looking too well, and my wife said once, Those Indians never say much. But they did, kids laughing and hollering, and the older ones talking among themselves, probably arguing too, and people see people only in a certain way, the way they want to see them.

Here I was watching the two men, wondering what they were up to and wondering too what I was up to. Hiding, like I said. The old one had a bundle in his hand, sticks and feathers wrapped up in cornhusks it looked like. They'd gone over by a rock that was split in half, a great huge rock even the halves were big. They were turned away from me and I couldn't see their fronts, and they stood by there for a long time. When the wind shifted towards me I could hear something. It was a kind of sing song, words, Indian words I suppose but spoke in a rhythm. Praying, that's what I figured; the Indians were praying by the rock split in halves. I couldn't stop looking at them and somehow I couldn't help feel that it was something fateful that I happened to be there.

I'd come up here just to be by myself because, well because I like the quiet and the thinking that I do and sort of studying things. I guess it's praying of a sort, yeah. And then it seemed like I was sort of part of what they were doing, like they wanted me to even though they didn't know I was there. The wind would change and drift the sound away and then bring it back, and it felt like I was part of that prayer that was going on. Something like that; it was an odd feeling and then not odd too.

When I was a boy in West Virginia, I'd look over the countryside and see how it was overturned by coalmining, and I would think of how it must have looked like before and still did in places. And I'd see something that was there, the meaning of something. That's what I was thinking now. The Indians I saw put those sticks and feathers down into the crack between the rocks, down in there somewhere, and then they stepped back and put their stuff together and said something to each other. And then they left. And then I watched them leave down the slope and I just felt, in fact I could see myself, like I was still hiding with the quiet and the mountain and that praying that had been going on.

Feathers

The father and his son found the little black and white kitten in the alley behind the Grasshopper Bookstore. Its fur was so fluffy and unruly that it looked like ruffled feathers, and so they named it Feathers.

"Feathers. Come here, Feathers," the father said, holding his hands out to the kitten. "Don't you think that's a good name?" he asked.

"He's got white circles around his eyes," his son said.

The father held the kitten gently in his hands. "It's kind of skinny. We should give it something when we get back to the apartment." The kitten was several weeks old, maybe five weeks. It might be able to eat a bit of something.

They took Feathers to the boy's and mother's apartment. No one was there, and they sat down on the doorstep. "I wonder where your mother is?" the father asked.

"She might have gone shopping," the boy said. He cradled Feathers in his arms. He kept looking into the kitten's eyes. It had very bright eyes which were now about to close into sleep.

"I hope she lets you keep it," the father said. "Remember that dog I brought you last summer, the puppy? She gave that away."

"The landlord didn't want pets around his apartments," the boy said. "So my mother gave it away."

"Maybe Feathers will be alright with this landlord. Kittens aren't much trouble," the father said.

The boy was very gentle with Feathers. He moved a hand very surely and carefully over the kitten which had fallen asleep. "I think we'll need a box for its poop," he said, "with sand in it."

"Yeah, it'll need that. Cats got a lot of that," the father said, chuckling.

The boy laughed, and he held the kitten away from him a moment just in case. Feather's eyes fell brightly open.

Looking at his son, the father wondered how his son was coming along, how he was learning things. He loved the boy who was now almost five years old, and it was hard not to dwell too much on the feeling of separation. He stroked the kitten with just the lightest touch of his finger tips.

"Maybe this summer you can come live with me for a while," the father said.

The boy didn't say anything for a moment, and then holding the kitten to his cheek, he said, "He's very warm. I can hear something inside of him."

"It's a she," the father said. "Feathers is a she, a girl kitten."

"Oh," his son said. And then he said, "I'm going to enroll in swimming class this summer. My mother said I could. It's over at the University."

"Well, you could still come and stay with me for a while."

At that moment, the boy's mother came home. She carried a couple of grocery bags. "Hello," she said, looking only briefly at her ex-husband. There were tiny beads of sweat on her forehead.

The boy's father got up from the doorstep and said, "Let me help you," offering his hands.

"No, that's alright," the boy's mother said. "It's so damned hot." She fumbled for her house key in her shoulder bag. Finding it, she began to unlock the door. Holding the bags in one arm and leaning into the screen door to prop it open, she couldn't fit the key into the hole. The key fell to the cement doorstep with a flat tinkle.

"Here, I'll get it for you," the boy's father said. He picked up the key and fitted it into the lock. He remembered very easily.

"David, hold this screen door open. Don't just stand there like that," the boy's mother said irritably. She stared fiercely at the kitten snuggled in the boy's arms, but only for a moment, and then she turned to enter the apartment.

For several minutes, the father stood at the door uneasily, not knowing what to do until she called from inside, "Come in. It's hot out there."

Stepping inside the apartment, he started to hang the key on the nail on the wall—as he had done out of habit in another place, in another time—and then he decided not to. "Here's your key," he said.

"Just hang it up," she snapped from the kitchen. "I'm trying to put stuff away. This house is a wreck." She banged things around in the kitchen.

Their son stayed outside. He had sat back down on the step and continued to study the kitten. Feathers had gone to sleep again.

"We found a kitten. David, show that kitten to your mother," he called through the screen door.

The boy's mother did not say anything, but she wasn't banging things around anymore.

David came inside and called into the kitchen, "He's got white circles around his eyes. His name is Feathers." And then he remembered and said, "I mean she," his voice trailing away.

"It's a she kitten," the mother said, an edge in her voice. She came into the living room with a magazine in her hand. She looked at her ex-husband and studied him for a half-moment. She held out the magazine and said, "This has something of yours in it."

"I know," he said. "I saw it." It was a regional magazine with gaudy color prints of Southwestern scenery.

"Oh, I guess you would have," she said and flipped the magazine casually on to an end table.

It was a poem that was in the magazine. One day in late fall a couple of years before, they had taken a ride into the mountains. He had followed a road indicated on a map which showed that the road led across the mountains and down the other side. They had driven up the mountainside, and the road became rougher and rougher until the ruts finally led nowhere.

They were forced to turn around. There was no way they could have driven over the mountains. They had seen an old house on the way back down. Only the walls were standing. The walls were of stone, no mortar, just stone, and the stones were balanced against the blue sky so fragilely.

"I want to feed Feathers," David said. The kitten was waking up.

"I think there's tuna in a bowl in the refrigerator. Maybe

she will eat a little of that. The kitten's kind of small yet, though."

"We found it behind the bookstore," the boy's father said. "It was just in the alley; maybe somebody lost it or abandoned it."

David brought a small dish of stale-looking tuna into the room. He set it down on the floor and put the kitten's nose to it. Feathers ignored it at first, and then she sniffed it and sniffed it again. Finally, the kitten licked it and began to nibble at the tuna. She did it with tiny deliberate nibbles.

The boy smiled and laughed happily as he said, "Mom, Dad, look, he's eating. He's eating the tuna. I mean she." He squatted by the kitten and looked on with amazement. Feathers did not seem to pay any mind to being the center of attention focused upon her by the father, mother, and son.

3 Women

"I'm gonna kill him," Rowena said. She wrenched the wheel sharply from the street into the lot by the launderette. "That son-of-a-bitch!" Her teeth ground down on her words.

Annie braced her hand on the dashboard; she didn't say anything.

The pickup truck tires spun gravel to the side as tires turned and they parked abruptly.

"That's the last stupid time he's gonna do that, the last." And then Rowena gripped the wheel hard for a half moment, let go, and jumped out of the truck.

Annie closed the door on her side and began to get their baskets of washing out of the truck bed. "We have so much laundry this time," she said.

Her sister threw her a glare that Annie could feel on her face. She almost dropped the bleach.

Rowena took the heaviest basket of clothes and lunged with its weight against the launderette door, almost knocking over the manager who was moving to open it for her. Annie murmured, "Sorry." Rowena didn't even notice.

They went back out one more time to get two more basket loads, and then they began to stuff empty washers. It was hot and steamy in the launderette. Rowena didn't say anything as she threw Ray's oil and grease grimed work clothes into a separate washer. As Annie put the checkered and stripes into another, she could see her sister's jaw muscles tensing and untensing.

"There," Annie said with a sigh when all the clothes were in. She was sweating and she could feel the biting odor of clorox at her nostrils. She knew she would feel nauseated soon and she would fight it as she always did.

When they finished putting the detergent into the top loading washers, Annie asked, "Do you want a coke? I'm going to have one; it's so hot in here."

Rowena didn't seem to hear at first but she finally said, "Yeah, I guess so," and sank down in a metal chair propped against the dull green wall. Annie brought back the cans of coke and handed one to her sister. They sat in silence.

The din was always the same in the launderette. Sloshing water, the change in cycles, wash spin rinse, the whirr of the dryers. Tin doors slamming, kids stamping their shoes on the cement floor, Okie and Navajo women talking. Annie could feel the nausea coming on. She sipped on her coke, trying to keep the sickly feeling down.

"You know I married that man because I loved him," Rowena said suddenly. She looked at Annie and then across the room. "I sure as hell did; I don't remember why but I did."

Annie nodded. She remembered how proud her sister had acted riding around in Ray's car. She sometimes went with them to the movies or to the store, and she always rode in the back seat.

"We were doing it all the way before we got married—did you know that?—because I loved him. The son-of-a-bitch." It was a matter of fact, the way Rowena said it.

Annie didn't know if it was a real question she was being asked but when Rowena looked at her, she said, "No, I didn't know." Her voice was even smaller than usual.

"It wasn't any great shakes," Rowena said, shrugging her shoulders, "and it wasn't going to make any difference because I wanted to get married. Now, it doesn't make any damn difference because I want to get out!" Her latter words were grim and final.

Not knowing if she should say anything, if there was anything to say, Annie found herself saying, "He loved you too. He told me."

"That bastard couldn't love anybody," Rowena said and then asked directly, "Did he say that?"

Annie hesitated and then said, "Yes." It was twice he had said so and she felt uneasy remembering the second time. She wished she hadn't mentioned it and feebly hoped Rowena would not ask for details.

The noise in the launderette seemed to ebb and then immediately rise. Annie tried to think around the knot of nausea in her stomach, and, out of the corner of her eyes, she was relieved to see Rowena staring far away to the other side of the launderette.

Ray had been drinking that weekend and fighting with Rowena. He'd been working on something that was wrong with the truck they had. Annie, who lived nearby with their mother, was watering Rowena's garden as a favor; Rowena had taken the kids to a church youth picnic that afternoon.

She knew they had been fighting. She could feel it when they did; she had heard yelling and then the car engine racing away. A half hour later, after lunch, she had started to water the garden. She was almost through when Ray turned from the truck and spoke to her.

"Your sister is nuts. No offense, but she's nuts," he said.

Annie had to giggle at that. Sometimes she said and felt the same as Ray had said about Rowena. But she didn't say anything.

"She wanted me to go to a picnic with her and the kids, and she got mad because I said I couldn't because I have to work on the truck so I can go to work in it tomorrow." Ray wiped his hands on a rag from an old t-shirt. And he lit a cigarette.

"The boys said you were all going to go," Annie said. Her nephews, who liked to talk with her, had been excited about the picnic.

"Well shoot, yeah, I was going to go, but then I couldn't. I can't help it if this old thing needs working on." He slammed his hand on the truck fender.

"I guess they'll be gone all afternoon," Annie said.

"I was going to go," Ray repeated, "but then I couldn't. Rowena said I was just making it up. I told her, 'You take that truck then and see how far it'll take you.' She said, 'Yeah, it'll take you as far as the bar, I know that much! It always does.' 'It takes me to work,' I said."

He threw away his cigarette and said, "She started yelling about my drinking. I told her not to yell so much. Shoot, you probably heard her over at your mother's." He looked at Annie.

"Yes. I heard both of you," she said, feeling a stir in herself for her sister. Rowena had talked, though not a lot, about Ray's drinking. It seemed to be other things besides the drinking but drinking had some to do with the other things also.

"I drink, sure, but I work steady, and we manage to get things. Sometimes she wants to get things that we can't afford, and we get into hassles about that too. Like that color TV, you know? I don't even like TV that much but she wanted to get it."

Rowena had been proud of the new console when they first bought it. She brought Annie and Mother over to see it and she kept putting lemony smelling polish on it although it didn't seem to need it. Lately though, Annie noticed that dust was gathering on the console top.

"Hassles," Ray said and shrugged, "but that's married life I guess. Annie, I love her but something's not there. I don't even know if it's love anymore. Maybe it's just a used-to-be love. What do you think about that." And he laughed in the boyish manner he had. He could tease, and Annie remembered before the marriage she used to laugh at his teasing. They all did. She couldn't help giggling now.

"I don't need used-to-be love, I need some right-now loving," Ray said, and laughing he suddenly took Annie's hand and squeezed it. For a split second, Annie felt a surge of sensual energy—and then she tried to withdraw her hand. Ray's hand-hold was strong and she had to jerk her hand from his. His laughter cut short and he looked startled.

Annie turned back to watering the rest of the lettuce and carrots. After she turned off the water and coiled the plastic hose, she walked to Ray who was cleaning parts in a can. She told him, "Rowena loves you too, Ray. It's not a used-to-be either. She worries; that's why she gets mad—crazy, like you say."

She had spoken without thinking much about what she said. She didn't know if Rowena loved him. If she had paused in thought she might not have said it. It was certain though that Rowena worried about their sons and herself and Ray.

Ray didn't say anything.

Rowena got up from the metal chair and threw the empty coke can into a trash container with a loud clatter. Annie could see that two of the top loading washers they had filled were in the rinse cycle. And then she looked at Rowena who was standing, staring at a woman who had just come in with a large cardboard box overflowing with clothes.

Rowena kept staring at the woman who held her gaze down as she found an empty washer right next to them. All other washers were full. The woman lifted her face and seemed to look frantically around the launderette but there were no other washers empty.

The woman sat her cardboard box down heavily, and Rowena sat back in the metal chair, watching the woman go out the door. After a moment, the woman came back through the launderette door with a pillow sack and still keeping her head down she began to put clothes into the single empty washer.

Annie noticed then the purple puffiness of the woman's white face. The dark swelling was mostly visible around her eyes and on the side of her neck. Annie sucked in her breath suddenly and Rowena looked at her. Annie said, "That woman, her face." "I saw," Rowena said, gruffly, just above her breath.

Without wanting to, trying at the same time not to, the sisters watched the woman. She looked totally wearied. Annie felt a shiver in her own bones and muscles. She noticed that some pieces of clothing the woman was stuffing into the washer had dark stains. The woman's upper lip glistened with sweat. She seemed to be near collapse and she stumbled as she reached into the cardboard box. Rowena jumped up and walked over.

"Let me help you," she said.

The woman had one hand on the edge of the washer; her knuckles were white. "No, that's alright," she said, stammering, "I'll get it done." And she pushed Rowena's hand away, almost slapping it.

"Okay," Rowena said, shrugged and started to walk away. She turned and said, gently, "We'll be finished with these four washers soon." The woman lifted her face an instant and nodded. Rowena sat down.

Not looking at Annie, she said, "She must have a bastard of an old man too." And then she spoke to herself, "I think I'm gonna get out of it. I know it'll upset Mother, but she doesn't know what I've gone through."

Annie didn't say anything right away and then she said, "She knows some. And she'll understand." She was trying to keep the muscles in her stomach from tensing with nausea but the more she tried the more it wanted to come.

Rowena turned to her. Very directly, she asked, "Do you understand?"

Feeling defensively small, Annie said, "No, not a lot." She glanced at the woman by the washer.

"To tell you the truth, I don't either," Rowena said. "I told you I loved—or did— Ray, but I want to get out. I'm convinced of that. It doesn't feel good anymore. Maybe it hasn't for a long time, and it's not safe for me anymore, nor for the boys. I don't know what he's going to do from one day to the next." She let her voice drift away.

The sisters were silent for several minutes each in their own minds. Annie's thoughts were mixed with the constant noise of the launderette and her nausea. She wondered, almost doing so aloud, if Rowena had the same sickening feelings. She had to get up and move around. "This one is just about to finish," she said. The spin light was on.

For several minutes, the woman had been standing by the washer she had started. She looked dazed—as if she did not know where she was. Annie couldn't help it as she said, "Please, won't you sit down." She pointed to the metal chair she had been sitting in.

The woman's red-tinged eyes locked on Annie's and Annie was about to feel an automatic wish that she hadn't said anything when the woman said, "Yes, I think I will." She took the few steps over to the chair and unsteadily sat down beside Rowena.

The first top loader finished spinning. Annie brought a wheeled basket over from the corner and she began to take the heavy wet clothes out. As she pulled handfuls out of the washer, Rowena came up beside her and said, "I can't stand it. It's done. I feel like I'm going nuts, and I know I'm not nuts. It's done. That woman just decided for me."

Annie looked at her sister's face and saw she had made a decision. She looked at the woman sitting tired and slumped on the metal chair. Her face was down again and she could see her lips moving. She was talking to herself or praying, and it could have been both.

The other washers stopped almost all at the same time and Rowena started to empty the one nearest the washer the woman had filled. When she finished, she turned and told the woman, "This one is free now, and I'll be done with this other real quick." She pointed to the one with Ray's clothes in it. The woman turned to Rowena. "Thank you," she said.

Before Rowena turned back to empty the washer, she said, "It'll be alright." Annie heard her say that and when she looked at the woman rising from the metal chair and at Rowena she found a shared faint smile on their faces.

Distance

George had been bought from Macario, a Mexican farmer, who lived five miles south of San Rafael.

"That goat is mean like Macario," the father said, trying to soothe the little girl, his daughter.

The girl was crying. She had just been butted and knocked down by George and her knee was scraped. Her father was cleaning her scrape with a clean cloth and a basin of cold water.

"We'll get that old goat tamed down," the father said.

George was a lively two-year-old billy buck. He was boss of the other goats. Now, he defiantly stood by a corner of the goat shed and watched the father and daughter.

The girl's father roped George the next day and tied him to a post just out of reach of the water trough. All the other goats and chickens and the couple of ducks were getting water, but George couldn't. It was a hot day.

At first, George didn't seem to pay any mind to not having any water. He just ignored it. In fact, he seemed to ignore the rope around his neck too. He laid down by the post and looked straight ahead. Once in a while, he would turn his head and look around very calmly. It grew hotter by mid-afternoon.

When the late afternoon shadows began to fall longer, the father put water in the trough for the other goats and he filled the bowls for the chickens and ducks. George got up on his legs then and for the first time he strained against the rope. He looked disdainfully at the rope and post and shook his bearded head and then he laid back down.

George watched the man for a moment and then he ignored him. He laid with his hooves drawn up under him.

"We're fixing that Mexican goat good," the father said at supper. The little girl looked out the kitchen window but she couldn't see the goat.

She had watched George during the day. She felt a tinge of pity for the goat but her knee still hurt and she remembered the cool water and her father's soothing voice.

The next morning when the girl saw George he was standing, and he was leaning, pulling at the end of the rope tied at the back of his neck. George pawed the ground as if he was trying to pull it like a rug towards him.

The other goats were let out of their shed; they drank water, were fed, and they wandered around looking for shade to lie in. George watched them enviously. He looked over at the man's house but no one was around. It was very hot again.

But midafternoon, the goat was lying down again. He laid with his head in the narrow strip of shade made by the post. His flanks were grown sunken and he was breathing rapidly. Once in a while, George raised his head and bleated forlornly and then he was quiet.

George looked sad and tired, the little girl thought when she saw the goat and wanted to tell her father. But her father wasn't around and that morning he had said, "We'll teach that old goat something alright!"

All the goats were accounted for before they were closed in for the night. George jumped up eagerly. He bleated out to the girl's father but he just ignored George. Even the other goats seemed to be ignoring him too.

The next day was the same and this time by noon, George was plainly in weak shape. His slick coat was mussed, the stiff hairs lying every which way, like a badly wired bale of hay. The girl had come to gather eggs at noon, and she watched George looking at her. On shaky legs, George had bleated, and the sound was pleading.

At their noon meal, the girl said, "When are you going to let George loose, Daddy?" The father looked at his little girl, smiled, and said, "When George learns, sweetheart, learns not to be so mean."

There was a dry spell that summer and the hot days that George was tied to the post burned. Little tufts of white clouds started up at the horizon in the mornings but they never worked together to even promise rain. The wind blew hotly, even the shades of farm buildings seemed to be no haven. George laid on the ground all the time now, and he leaned with his spine against the post like he was trying to draw some strength from it.

By morning of the fifth day, George hardly moved at all. The goat was lying on its side heaving great weak breaths infrequently. There were shallow gnaw marks on the dry wooden post. The girl's father checked the rope that held the goat. The strong rope still held George very securely.

The girl watched her father as he watered and fed the other animals. For several moments she was hopeful that he would turn from his duties and take his knife and cut the rope that held George. But her father walked away and started to do something else; he didn't look at George anymore.

When evening came, the father penned the animals up. He checked George and found the goat's eyes clear, not sickly. But he needed water and food—he even spoke to George. George's eyes stared straight ahead, not giving the slightest flicker of recognition.

The night of the fifth day there was a full moon. Out the window of her bedroom, the girl could see very clearly. She could see the white flanks of the hills a mile away. She could see the dark tufts of trees on the hillsides.

She looked at the goat shed. And then she could see the post that stood in an open space near the shed. The moon was very bright and the post was white and shiney. At the foot of the post, in the very clear light of the moon, was a shadow. It was very still. And she grew afraid.

The girl crawled back into her covers but it was hot and stifling and she threw back the covers and covered her eyes with her hands. She couldn't sleep. She listened. Except for the crickets in the summer night, it was very quiet.

The girl got out of bed and dressed quickly. She hadn't put on her shoes and it was painful from pebbles and debris to make her way hurriedly to George. The light from the moon slanted into George's eyes and made them shine with a sorrowful odd light. He weakly raised his head and looked at her.

She gave out a small cry then and reached for the knot around the goat's neck. The rope was so tightly knotted it was impossible to undo. She tried the knot at the post until her fingers bled but there was no way to undo it. Finally, she could only whisper, I'm sorry, I'm sorry, holding the rope in her hands.

In the morning at breakfast, her father said, "I'm going to let George go today and see if he behaves any better." The girl was overjoyed, and after she had helped her mother with the breakfast dishes, she ran to the goat shed. George was still there. He wasn't tied to the post. He was just there.

The goat's breathing was trembly and loose. It was like a weak wind, purposeless and uncertain. It's eyes were half shut.

"What's wrong with George? Why won't he get up?" the girl asked her father who was standing nearby.

Not looking at her, he said, "He'll get up when he gets thirsty and hungry." There didn't seem to be any hope in his voice. A pan of water stood at George's head. The goat just lay there not moving.

The little girl began to cry then aloud and her father came to her and began to wipe her tears from her face. As he looked into his daughter's eyes he saw them looking fiercely into his and past him and into a great distance beyond them.

Kaiser and the War

Kaiser got out of the state pen when I was in the fourth grade. I don't know why people called him Kaiser. Some called him Hitler too, since he was Kaiser, but I don't think he cared at all what they called him. He was probably just glad to get out of the state pen.

Kaiser got into the state pen because he didn't go into the army. That's what my father said anyway, and because he was a crazy nut, according to some people, which was probably why he didn't want to go into the army in the first place, which was what my father said also.

The army wanted him anyway, or maybe they didn't know he was crazy or supposed to be. They came for him out at home on the reservation, and he said he wasn't going to go because he didn't speak good English. Kaiser didn't go to school more than just the first or second grade. He said what he said in Indian and his sister said it in English for him. The army men, somebody from the county draft board, said they'd teach him English, don't worry about it, and how to read and write and give him clothes and money when he got out of the army so that he could start regular as any American. Just like anybody else, and they threw in stuff about how it would be good for our tribe and the people of the U.S.A.

Well, Kaiser, who didn't understand that much English anyway, listened quietly to his sister telling him what the army draft-board men were saying. He didn't ask any questions, just once in a while said, "Yes," like he'd been taught to say in the first grade. Maybe some of the interpretation was lost the way his sister was doing it, or maybe he went nuts like some people said he did once in a while because the next thing he did was to bust out the door and start running for Black Mesa.

The draft-board men didn't say anything at first, and then they got pretty mad. Kaiser's sister cried because she didn't want Kaiser to go into the army, but she didn't want him running out just like that either. She had gone to the Indian school in Albuquerque, and she had learned that stuff about patriotism, duty, honor—even if you were said to be crazy.

At about that time, their grandfather, Faustin, cussed in Indian at the draft-board men. Nobody had noticed when he came into the house, but there he was, fierce-looking as hell as usual, although he wasn't fierce at all. Then he got mad at his granddaughter and the men, asked what they were doing in his house, making the women cry and not even sitting down like friendly people did. Old Faustin and the army confronted each other. The army men were confused and getting more and more nervous. The old man told the girl to go out of the room, and he'd talk to the army himself, although he didn't speak a word of English except "goddammey," which didn't sound too much like English but he threw it in once in a while anyway.

Those army men tried to get the girl to come back, but the old man wouldn't let her. He told her to get to grinding corn or something useful. They tried sign language, and when Faustin figured out what they were waving their hands around for, he laughed out loud. He wouldn't even take the cigarettes offered him, so the army men didn't say anything more. The last thing they did, though, was give the old man a paper, but they didn't explain what it was for. They probably hoped it would get read somehow.

Well, after they left, the paper did get read by the girl, and she told Faustin what it was about. The law was going to come and take Kaiser to jail because he wouldn't go into the army by himself. Grandfather Faustin sat down and talked quietly to himself for a while and then he got up to look for Kaiser.

Kaiser was on his way home by then, and his grandfather told him what was going to happen. They sat down by the side of the road and started to make plans. Kaiser would go hide up on Black Mesa and maybe go all the way to Brushy Mountain if the law really came to poking around seriously. Faustin would take him food and tell him the news once in a while.

Everybody in the village knew what was going on pretty soon. Some approved, and some didn't. Some thought it was pretty funny. My father, who couldn't go in the army even if he wanted to because there were too many of us kids, laughed about it for days. The people who approved of it and thought it funny were the ones who knew Kaiser was crazy and that the army must be even crazier. The ones who disapproved were mostly those who were scared of him. A lot of them were the parents or brother of girls who they must have suspected of liking Kaiser. Kaiser was pretty good-looking and funny in the way he talked for a crazy guy. And he was a hard worker. He worked every day out in the fields or up at the sheep camp for his parents while they were alive and for his sister and nephew and grandfather. These people, who were scared of him and said he should have gone into the army perhaps it'll do him good, didn't want him messing around their daughters or sisters, which they said he did from time to time. Mostly these people were scared he would do *something*, and there was one too many nuts around in the village anyway, they said.

My old man didn't care though. He was buddies with Kaiser. When there was a corn dance up at the community hall they would have a whole lot of fun singing and laughing and joking, and once in a while when someone brought around a bottle or two they would really get going and the officers of the tribe would have to warn them to behave themselves.

Kaiser was O.K. though. He came around home quite a lot. His own kinfolks didn't care for him too much because he was crazy, and they didn't go out of their way to invite him to eat or spend the night when he dropped by their homes and it happened to get dark before he left. My mother didn't mind him around. When she served him something to eat, she didn't act like he was nuts, or supposed to be; she just served him and fussed over him like he was a kid, which Kaiser acted like a lot of the time. I guess she didn't figure a guy who acted like a kid was crazy.

Right after we finished eating, if it happened to be supper, my own grandfather, who was a medicine man, would talk to him and to all of us kids who were usually paying only half attention. He would tell us advice, about how the world was, how each person, everything, was important. And then he would tell us stories about the olden times. Legends mostly, about the *katzina*, Spider Woman, where our *hano*, people came from. Some of the stories were funny, some sad, and some pretty boring. Kaiser would sit there, not saying anything except "*Eheh*," which is what you're supposed to say once in a while to show that you're listening to the olden times.

After half of us kids were asleep, Grandfather would quit talking, only Kaiser wouldn't want him to quit and he'd ask for more, but Grandfather wouldn't tell any more. What Kaiser would do was start telling himself about the olden times. He'd lie on the floor in the dark, or sometimes up on the roof which was where he'd sleep in the summer, talking. And sometimes he'd sing, which is also part of the old times. I would drift off to sleep just listening to him.

Well, he didn't come around home after he went up on Black Mesa. He just went up there and stayed there. The law, which was the County Sheriff, an officer, and the Indian Agent from the Indian Affairs office in Albuquerque, came out to get him, but nobody would tell them where he was. The law had a general idea where he was, but that didn't get them very far because they didn't know the country around Black Mesa. It's rougher than hell up there, just a couple of sheep camps in a lot of country.

The Indian Agent had written a letter to the officers of the tribe that they would come up for Kaiser on a certain day. There were a lot of people waiting for them when they drove up to the community meeting hall. The County Sheriff had a bulging belly and he had a six-shooter strapped to his hip. When the men standing outside the community hall saw him step out of the government car, they made jokes. Just like the Lone Ranger, someone said. The law didn't know what they were laughing about, and they said, Hello, and paid no attention to what they couldn't understand.

Faustin was among them. But he was silent and he smoked a roll-your-own. The Agent stopped before him, and Faustin took a slow drag on his roll-your-own but didn't look at the man.

"Faustin, my old friend," the Agent said. "How are you?"

The old man didn't say anything. He let the tobacco smoke out slowly and looked straight ahead. Someone in the crowd told Faustin what the Agent had said, but the old man didn't say anything at all.

The law thought he was praying or that he was a wise man contemplating his answer, the way he was so solemn-like, so they didn't press him. What Faustin was doing was ignoring the law. He didn't want them to talk with him. He turned to a man at his side.

"Tell this man I do not want to talk. I can't understand what they're saying in American anyway. And I don't want anyone to tell me what they say. I'm not interested." He looked at the government then, and he dismissed their presence with his indignation.

"The old man isn't gonna talk to you." someone said.

The Agent and Sheriff Big Belly glared at the man. "Who's in charge around here?" the Sheriff said.

The Indians laughed. They joked by calling each other big belly. The Governor of the tribe and two chiefs came soon. They greeted the law, and then they went into the meeting hall to confer about Kaiser.

"Well, have you brought Kaiser?" the Indian Agent asked, although he saw that they hadn't and knew that they wouldn't.

"No," the Governor said. And someone translated for him. "He will not come."

"Well, why don't you bring him? If he doesn't want to come, why don't you bring him. A bunch of you can bring him," the Agent said. He was becoming irritated.

The Governor, chiefs, and men talked to each other. One old man held the floor a while, until others got tired of him telling about the old times and how it was and how the Americans had said a certain thing and did another and so forth. Someone said, "We can bring him. Kaiser should come by himself anyway. Let's go get him." He was a man who didn't like Kaiser. He looked around carefully when he got through speaking and sat down.

"Tell the Americans that is not the way," one of the chiefs said. "If our son wants to meet these men he will come." And the law was answered with the translation.

"I'll be a son-of-a-bitch," the Sheriff said, and the Indians laughed quietly. He glared at them and they stopped. "Let's go get him ourselves," he continued.

The man who had been interpreting said, "He is crazy."

"Who's crazy?" the Sheriff yelled, like he was refuting an accusation. "I think you're all crazy."

"Kaiser, I think he is crazy," the interpreter said like he was ashamed of saying so. He stepped back, embarrassed.

Faustin then came to the front. Although he said he didn't want to talk with the law, he shouted. "Go get Kaiser yourself. If he's crazy, I hope he kills you. Go get him."

"O.K.," the Agent said when the interpreter finished. "We'll go get him ourselves. Where is he?" The Agent knew no one would tell him, but he asked it anyway.

With that, the Indians assumed the business that the law came to do was over, and that the law had resolved what it came to do in the first place. The Indians began to leave.

"Wait," the Agent said. "We need someone to go with us. He's up on Black Mesa, but we need someone to show us where."

The men kept on leaving. "We'll pay you. The government will pay you to go with us. You're deputized," the Agent said. "Stop them, Sheriff," he said to the County Sheriff, and the Sheriff yelled, "Stop, come back here," and put a hand to his six-shooter. When he yelled, some of the Indians looked at him to laugh. He sure looked funny and talked funny. But some of them came back. "All right, you're deputies, you'll get paid," the Sheriff said. Some of them knew what that meant, others weren't too sure. Some of them decided they'd come along for the fun of it.

The law and the Indians piled into the government car and a pickup truck which belonged to one of the deputies who was assured that he would get paid more than the others.

Black Mesa is fifteen miles back on the reservation. There are dirt roads up to it, but they aren't very good; nobody uses them except sheepherders and hunters in the fall. Kaiser knew what he was doing when he went up there, and he probably saw them when they were coming. But it wouldn't have made any difference, because when the law and the deputies came up to the foot of the mesa they still weren't getting anywhere. The deputies, who were still Indians, wouldn't tell or didn't really know where Kaiser was at the moment. So they sat for a couple of hours at the foot of the mesa, debating what should be done. The law tried to get the deputies to talk. The Sheriff was boiling mad by this time, getting madder too, and he was for *persuading* one of the deputies into telling where Kaiser was exactly. But he reasoned the deputy wouldn't talk, being that he was Indian too, and so he shut up for a while. He had figured out why the Indians laughed so frequently even though it was not as loud as before they were deputized.

Finally, they decided to walk up Black Mesa. It's rough going, and when they didn't know which was the best way to go up they found it was even rougher. The real law dropped back one by one to rest on a rock or under a piñon tree until only the deputies were left. They watched the officer from the Indian Affairs office sitting on a fallen log some yards back. He was the last one to keep up so far, and he was unlacing his shoes. The deputies waited patiently for him to start again and for the others to catch up.

"It's sure hot," one of the deputies said.

"Yes, maybe it'll rain soon," another said.

"No, it rained for the last time last month. Maybe next year."

"Snow then," another said.

They watched the Sheriff and the Indian Agent walking toward them half a mile back. One of them limped.

"Maybe the Americans need a rest," someone said. "We walked a long ways."

"Yes, they might be tired," another said. "I'll go tell that one that we're going to stop to rest," he said, and walked back to the law sitting on the log. "We gonna stop to rest," he told the law. The law didn't say anything as he massaged his feet. And the deputy walked away to join the others.

They didn't find Kaiser that day or the next day. The deputies said they could walk all over the mesa without finding him for all eternity, but they wouldn't find him. They didn't mind walking, they said. As long as they got paid for their time. Their crops were already in, and they'd just hire someone to haul winter wood for them now that they had the money. But they refused to talk. The ones who wanted to tell where Kaiser was, if they knew, didn't say so out loud, but they didn't tell anyway so it didn't make any difference. They were too persuaded by the newly found prosperity of employment.

The Sheriff, exhausted by the middle of the second day of walking the mesa, began to sound like he was for going back to Albuquerque. Maybe Kaiser'd come in by himself; he didn't see any sense in looking for some Indian anyway just to get him into the army. Besides, he'd heard the Indian was crazy. When the Sheriff had first learned the Indian's name was Kaiser he couldn't believe it, but he was assured that wasn't his real name, just something he was called because he was crazy. But the Sheriff didn't feel any better or less tired, and he was getting jumpy about the crazy part.

At the end of the second day, the law decided to leave. Maybe we'll come back, they said. We'll have to talk this over with the Indian Affairs officials. Maybe it'll be all right if that Indian doesn't have to be in the army after all. And they left. The Sheriff, his six-shooter off his hip now, was pretty tired out, and he didn't say anything.

The officials for the Indian Affairs didn't give up though. They sent back some more men. The County Sheriff decided it wasn't worth it; besides, he had a whole county to take care of. And the Indians were deputized again. More of them volunteered this time; some had to be turned away. They had figured out how to work it; they wouldn't have to tell, if they knew, where Kaiser was. All they would have to do was walk and say from time to time, "Maybe he's over there by that canyon. Used to be there was some good hiding places back when the Apache and Navajo were raising hell." And some would go over there and some in the other direction, investigating good hiding places. But after camping around Black Mesa for a week this time, the Indian Affairs gave up. They went by Faustin's house the day they left for Albuquerque and left a message: the government would wait, and when Kaiser least expected it, they would get him and he would have to go to jail.

Kaiser decided to volunteer for the army. He had decided to after he had watched the law and the deputies walk all over the mesa. Grandfather Faustin had come to visit him up at one of the sheep camps, and the old man gave him all the news at home, and then he told Kaiser the message the government had left.

"O.K.," Kaiser said. And he was silent for a while and

nodded his head slowly like his grandfather did. "I'll join the army."

"No," his grandfather said. "I don't want you to. I will not allow you."

"Grandfather, I do not have to mind you. If you were my grandfather or uncle on my mother's side, I would listen to you and probably obey you, but you are not, and so I will not obey you."

"You are really crazy then," Grandfather Faustin said. "If that's what you want to do, go ahead." He was angry and he was sad, and he got up and put his hand on his grandson's shoulder and blessed him in the people's way. After that the old man left. It was in the evening when he left the sheep camp, and he walked for a long time away from Black Mesa before he started to sing.

The next day, Kaiser showed up at home. He ate with us, and after we ate we sat in the living room with my grandfather.

"So you've decided to go into the Americans' army," my grandfather said. None of us kids, nor even my parents, had known he was going, but my grandfather had known all along. He probably knew as soon as Kaiser had walked into the house. Maybe even before that.

My grandfather blessed him then, just like Faustin had done, and he talked to him of how a man should behave and what he should expect. Just general things, and Grandfather turned sternly toward us kids, who were playing around as usual. My father and mother talked with him too, and when they were through, my grandfather put corn meal in Kaiser's hand for him to pray with. Our parents told us kids to tell Kaiser goodbye and good luck, and after we did he left.

The next thing we heard was that Kaiser was in the state pen.

Later on, some people went to visit him up at the state pen. He was O.K. and getting fat, they said, and he was getting on O.K. with everybody, the warden told them. And when someone had asked Kaiser if he was O.K., he said he was fine and he guessed he would be American pretty soon, being that he was around them so much. The people left Kaiser some home-baked bread and dried meat and came home after being assured by the warden that he'd get out pretty soon, maybe right after the war. Kaiser was a model inmate. When the visitors got home to the reservation, they went and told Faustin his grandson was O.K., getting fat and happy as any American. Old Faustin didn't have anything to say about that.

Well, the war was over after a while. Faustin died sometime near the end of it. Nobody had heard him mention Kaiser at all. Kaiser's sister and nephew were the only ones left at their home. Sometimes someone would ask about Kaiser, and his sister or nephew would say, "Oh, he's fine. He'll be home pretty soon. Right after the war." But after the war was over, they just said he was fine.

My father and a couple of other guys went down to the Indian Affairs office to see what they could find out about Kaiser. They were told that Kaiser was going to stay in the pen longer now because he had tried to kill somebody. Well, he just went crazy one day, and he made a mistake, so he'll just have to stay in for a couple of more years or so, the Indian Affairs said. That was the first anybody heard of Kaiser trying to kill somebody, and some people said why the hell didn't they put him in the army for that like they wanted to in the first place. So Kaiser remained in the pen long after the war was over, and most of the guys who had gone into the army from the tribe had come home. When he was due to get out, the Indian Affairs sent a letter to the Governor, and several men from the village went to get him.

My father said Kaiser was quiet all the way home on the bus. Some of the guys tried to joke with him, but he just wouldn't laugh or say anything. When they got off the bus at the highway and began to walk home, the guys broke into song, but that didn't bring Kaiser around. He kept walking quiet and reserved in his gray suit. Someone joked that Kaiser probably owned the only suit in the whole tribe.

"You lucky so-and-so. You look like a rich man," the joker said. The others looked at him sharply and he quit joking, but Kaiser didn't say anything.

When they reached his home, his sister and nephew were very happy to see him. They cried and laughed at the same time, but Kaiser didn't do anything except sit at the kitchen table and look around. My father and the other guys gave him advice and welcomed him home again and left.

After that, Kaiser always wore his gray suit. Every time you saw him he was wearing it. Out in the fields or at the plaza watching the *katzina*, he wore the suit. He didn't talk much any more, my father said, and he didn't come around home any more either. The suit was getting all beat-up looking, but he just kept on wearing it so that some people began to say that he was showing off.

"That Kaiser," they said, "he's always wearing his suit, just like he was an American or something. Who does he think he is anyway?" And they'd snicker, looking at Kaiser with a sort of envy. Even when the suit was torn and soiled so that it hardly looked anything like a suit, Kaiser wore it. And some people said, "When he dies, Kaiser is going to be wearing his suit." And they said that like they wished they had gotten a suit like Kaiser's.

Well, Kaiser died, but without his gray suit. He died up at one of his distant relative's sheep camps one winter. When someone asked about the suit, they were told by Kaiser's sister that it was rolled up in some newspaper at their home. She said that Kaiser had told her, before he went up to the sheep camp, that she was to send it to the government. But, she said, she couldn't figure out what he meant, whether Kaiser had meant the law or somebody, maybe the state pen or the Indian Affairs.

The person who asked about the suit wondered about Kaiser's instructions. He couldn't figure out why Kaiser wanted to send a beat-up suit back. And then he figured, Well, maybe that's the way it was when you either went into the state pen or the army and became an American.

Pennstuwehniyaahtsi:
Quuti's Story

Quuti told me this story, Santiago said to Cholly, his 12-year old grandson, as they walked from their sheep camp in the mountain canyon to the Pueblo. I don't know how much of it is true but there are true things in it. He told it to me some years ago and it is about a time long before that, perhaps when I was a little boy.

Quuti was already no longer a child when he was taken by some white people who were teachers of the belief of the Mericano. Quuti said, We had been told this would happen. My grandmother was in great fear of them. When they would come around, she would take us children up to the hills and wait until they left. But it was one day when we were not prepared that they came. Two of them in a buckboard and another on a horse.

They just simply took me. They had a piece of paper on which was written something that would take me. My grandmother and my father and mother protested but it was of no avail. They said our leaders had agreed; it was written in the paper. So I went. My family and I cried. My mother packed me something to eat, dried meat and bread, what little we had. My father gave me a cornmeal pouch which he told me to hide. The white people put me in the buckboard and off we went.

That evening we camped. We headed east but I didn't know then where we were although years later I did.

They built a fire and cooked something. I took my sack and started to eat my food but the woman grabbed it from me and threw it away. The coyotes probably ate it. I started to cry because I was afraid they meant to starve me; such things had happened to our people in captivity. I knew that from the stories told by elder people. The woman pulled me out of the buckboard and sat me down on the ground, and she gave me a bowl with mushy stuff, hard bread, and meat. I started to eat then as I was glad they weren't going to starve me, but the woman grabbed my hand and put a metal thing in my fingers and stuck it into the meat. She was talking to me but at that time I didn't understand a word of it.

The woman then showed me by using her metal thing to put food into her mouth. I tried but I was clumsy at it, and I thought it would take me all night to eat my supper. I learned that I didn't have to eat my bread with the thing which I learned later was called a fork. I guess I started learning then how the Mericano lived their lives.

It is much simpler, of course, and easier to eat with the fingers but they preferred to make it difficult. It makes them feel better, maybe more intelligent, maybe more skillful, to live such complicated lives, Quuti said.

Quuti said things like that about the Mericano, Santiago said. He said he learned so many unnecessary and pointless things at the place where he was taken to. But he went ahead and learned because it was required. I became a good Indian, he would say and laugh.

Let's stop for a while, Good Indian, Santiago said to Cholly, and they sat at the roadside on a large rock.

Where did they take him, Grandfather? Cholly wanted to know.

Well, after camp that night, they went to a large town where he was put on the train with other Indian children. Some were just babies, little, Quuti said. We were all sad as we looked out of the windows at the land flying away from us. Travelling for days and nights, we finally stopped and, later, after I learned some Mericano words I could name the place. Pennstu-wehniyaahtsi. It was a school there and that was the place where we were to learn how it was to live like the Mericano.

And they taught us or tried to, and we tried also because we had no choice. If we didn't we didn't get anything to eat, or we got locked up, or had to do hard extra work until our hands would bleed. Most of us learned how to speak in Mericano although it was hard to say the strange words. And to write it.

We could not speak our own languages because that was not allowed and because there was no one else who spoke similarly. We were all different peoples from each other. But we found ways, and we even learned to talk with each other in our own ways even if we would be punished when we got caught. Sometimes I would go to the barn and talk to the cows. They would just look at me, of course, but at least I could hear myself and I would not forget the sound of my own language. I surely must have told those cows a lot of stories.

Cholly and his grandfather walked the miles eastward toward the Pueblo, and there was no sound except the story, their footsteps, and the calls of crows once in a while.

I stayed at the school called Carlyle, Santiago said as Quuti had told them, for about three years. One day because I had learned I was fifteen years old, I decided that I had enough of the Mericano's teaching. I was already a man and I was still being treated as a child, and I was concerned that my parents needed my help. And I was worried—I thought about it a lot—that I was becoming more like the Mericano than one of our people.

So I told the person in charge of us, and he stared at me for a while and then said, William—that was my Mericano name— you are a good Indian boy and you're becoming a fine black-smith. It is a good trade; the United States needs skilled workers like you for we are going to be the greatest nation in the world. And I knew that I was never going to go home if I stayed in that Mericano place. So I decided that night I would leave.

I told this Chisheh from San Carlos I was leaving. He was younger than me and he cried but he wished me a good journey. That night we packed me some food and a few clothes, and he taught me a song which meant this: Run, the wind speeds you. Walk, the trees hide you. Speak, the birds hear you. Sing, your voice comforts you. It was a song his people sang in their fight against the Mericano soldiers.

So Quuti left Pennstuwehniyaahtsi, Santiago said. It must have been late autumn when he did because he got caught in a snow storm. Cholly noticed that the afternoon sun was nearing the horizon. They had walked for miles and Santiago had kept up the same rhythm, never seeming to strain, his arms and hands swinging and indicating points in Quuti's story.

I had walked for many days. A storm came suddenly, and I almost froze. Never had I seen anything like that. It felt like the wind was blowing me more steps backward than I took forward. Finally, I found a barn in which I took shelter. I had to pull ice from my hair. There were cows in that barn and they kept me from freezing. I think it was two days and nights that I stayed. The next morning the snow was as high as the door of the barn, and the wind was still blowing and bitter cold. I was afraid of the cold, and I was afraid of getting caught and sent back to the school.

I didn't know what I should do, but finally I decided I would find the people who owned the barn and cows and tell them the truth. I would tell them I was only on my way back to my people in the west, and I hoped they would have compassion and not report me to authorities. I was very hungry. After many many days of walking, I had run out of food, and I had only the cows milk for nourishment. And so I started to dig out of the barn.

I had managed to push the barn door open a little and had begun to dig for a while when I heard a sound, and I listened and it sounded like someone was digging too. And it was.

Suddenly, the snow fell open, and there was a man standing in front of me who was so startled he dropped his shovel. And then he said something, but I didn't understand. I thought the cold had frozen my ears and brain so I couldn't understand or I had so quickly forgotten the Mericano language. But I soon figured out it wasn't Mericano he was speaking; it was another language.

Anyway, I understood from his gestures that he had been digging a tunnel through the snow so he could get to the barn to see after his cows. He was worried about them and we went into the barn, and he was so glad to see they were alright he started to kiss them and hug them and rub their hides to warm them up. And talking to them in this strange language. And I knew he wasn't Mericano for I had never seen any of them act like this man.

He was smiling and laughing because he was so happy, and then he started to milk the cows whose teats were so full they must have been hurting. So I helped him. After we finished milking and fed the cows, he pulled me along to his house through the tunnel he had made in the snow. A wife and children were there and they all set to work in making me feel at home. I was still half frozen and I had on clothes that were worn and dirty.

The man put me into a tub of warm water and then I was fed. And all this time, they were talking to me but I couldn't understand them, and I said a few things in Mericano and they couldn't understand that either. So I said some things in our language too and it was all the same, and we got along just fine. I was happy to be warm and not hungry and freezing anymore, and they were kind, friendly, and compassionate.

I tried to explain from where I had been coming and where I was going but it didn't seem to make any impression at all. After a couple of days as I got my strength back, I wanted to leave but I owed that family something for saving my life and so I stayed for a few more days to help them out with their farm. I think by then the woman and man understood where I was headed and why, and they indicated they wanted to help but it seemed to them to be so far away where I was going and it was winter and fearfully cold.

Those people, they knew about journeys and difficulties, they got me to understand, and they asked me to stay until the winter was over. So I stayed until spring came. We never spoke any Mericano but I learned to speak their language a little, and they learned to speak a little of ours, especially the children, a boy and a girl. Their hair was so yellow it shone.

I have never forgotten them and their name. Yoonson. They were a fine and caring family. Yoonson. When I got married and my first son was born I called him that—Yoonson. That journey was hard but if it wasn't for those people I would have never made it home.

Cholly could see the smoke rising from chimneys in the Pueblo and he was glad for that. He was tired but Santiago still seemed to be walking strongly along. The wind was colder now and had started to pick up and the sun had dropped below the mountain ridge.

So Quuti arrived home safely, Santiago said, on that long journey, and I believe it is mostly true. Santiago smiled. Quuti was a fine and good man.

When they arrived home and were warming themselves by the kitchen stove, Santiago, smiling again, said to Cholly's mother, That son of yours is quite a walker. He nearly walked my poor legs off. I think he would have made old man, beloved Quuti, a good companion on his walk from Pennstuwehniyaahtsi.

What Indians Do

Alvin was talking about a play he is thinking of writing. He was describing this one character. "It's this old Eskimo uncle who is listening to one of his nephews talking about American scientists going out into space, exploring, you know, the unknown depths of space. And this old uncle says, 'But they don't know that they should look into the space that is in here.' " And Alvin motioned his hands and finger tips unto his chest like the Eskimo uncle.

Sometimes it's kind of difficult to explain about space inside of oneself. It is almost as if it were easier to talk about space which is outside, out there, away from oneself. Because of that it's often hard to answer convincingly enough a question such as this one asked by college student. "What do Indians do at a powwow anyway?" he asked.

John, a Sioux, who is the professor of the student said, "Well, there's dancing and singing and socializing. It's a social gathering with spiritual significance. There are formalized dances which only certain dancers can participate in and then there are others in which everyone can join. Come and see sometimes. Join in, sing, dance, you'll catch on. It's a sharing."

"Yeah, that's what happens," I offered. "It's like a story being told when it's not *only* being told. The storyteller doesn't just tell about the characters, what they did or said, what happens in the story and so on. No, he participates in the story with those who are listening. The listeners in the same way are taking part in the story. The story includes them in. You see, it's more like an event, the story telling. The story is not just a story then—it's occuring, coming into being."

Most people watch parades like they watch the movies. They may wish to join in but they don't. They watch TV the same way. The world of that box within the plastic box is so far away, removed from our ability to touch, to deal with, in fact.

Maybe it's better though; maybe it's safer. Maybe it is, but we don't learn much that way. We're too far away.

Sometime ago when my father said in our Acoma Pueblo language, "Yaaka Hano naitra guh," I suddenly didn't know what he was talking about. I grew up speaking our language and I have heard that announcement countless times. But I've also acquired some formal education in western linguistics and other strange practices, and so I didn't know what he was saying for a moment.

You see, "Yaaka Hano naitra guh," literally translates into, "Corn People will occur." Or happen. Figuratively, and in a conversational sense, it means that "The people of the Corn Clan will be putting on a dancing event." That's what my father said, but what he also meant, literally, was that the "Corn People will occur." Yaaka Hano naitra guh. The Corn Hano will be bringing that event into actuality. The dancing will be happening. The people will occur in the dancing event. They will come into being. They will give it life.

Why my analytical American education got me lost for a moment there was that I was looking into the square world of that box from so far away. I was watching and not participating in the event of my father speaking with me.

I liked Alvin's story about the old Eskimo uncle and in return I told him this one.

"A Laguna Pueblo friend was telling me about his Grandpa watching TV one time. The old man didn't understand English very much and his grandsons, two schoolboys, were telling him what was going on within the TV screen. The moon walk was happening. A man was chopping at a large moon boulder with a small pickaxe. The boys told their Grandpa, 'Those are Mericano scientists, Nana; the Mericano government spent three hundred million dollars to go to the moon. They are gathering those rocks to study them. They are looking for knowledge.'

"The Grandpa watched for a while and then he went outside to go to the outhouse. On his return home, he picked up a small rock, and then he went back inside. 'Grandsons,' he said to the boys watching the moonwalk, 'I have something in my hand and I want to show it to you.' He had his hand clenched like he held a secret surprise or a trick. The boys said, 'Ah, Grandpa, you're just going to trick us,' suspicious because Indian grandpas are famous for their trickery when it comes to their grandsons. 'No, I'm not going to trick you, Grandsons,' their Grandpa said. 'Okay then, Grandpa, what is it?' the boys said. And their Nana opened his hand. And the boys said, 'Ah, that's just a rock, Grandpa, you tricked us again.' 'No,' their Grandpa said with a chuckle, casting a glance at the TV, 'that's knowledge.' "

Alvin liked that story and his face looked like he was thinking about that Eskimo uncle looking into the space within himself.

One Sunday morning I got out of bed, and, as usual, one of the first things I did was take a look at the San Francisco Examiner. I ran headlong into this: "PRIVATE PROPERTY WEEK BEGINS TODAY." And then I had to read on. "The San Francisco Board of Realtors has decided to tell the truth about Uncle Sam."

I read on because I thought the Board of Realtors would tell the truth, but it didn't. I thought the Examiner would tell about U.S. corporations building suburbs outside of Albuquerque and Phoenix on Indian lands, taking what little water Indians have left. I thought it would tell about the Indians pocketed into leftover tiny enclaves in San Diego County. But, of course, it didn't.

The article in the Financial Section did say that Uncle Sam "was very much a real person, one Samuel P. Wilson, a Massachusetts meat packer who had the contract for supplying the American Army with beef during the War of 1812."

Yes, it did say that and it also said that the Board of Realtors is "distributing copies of the National Association of Realtor's book, *Uncle Sam, The Man, and the Legend*, to all local schools and branch libraries." They will, I am sure of that, and they will do as good a job as they do teaching "private property," but it will still not be the truth.

The weekend before, Roxanne and I heard an archeologist say, "Unfortunately, we have no control over what happens." We were discussing Interstate highways, Kennecott Copper, coal mines, power plants, land and water, and Indians. I had said, "You know what Indian people even wish sometimes? That archeologists would be really on our side." The archeologist, who works for the U.S. Forest Service, said, "Sometimes we coordinate with other Federal agencies like the Bureau of Indian Affairs." They don't have control over what happens.

In San Diego several days later, I was talking about this at a poetry reading, coming down not gently on Americanization. A Choctaw woman, who is a good friend, asked, "Do you have anything funny to read?" She meant other emphases and themes in my poetry, I think. She meant that power plants, multi-national corporations, and loss of Indian lands aren't funny.

Another friend, a Hopi man, asked me, "Do you ever get set upon by Indian people who question what you are teaching in Indian literature, by your writing I mean?" And he explained, "You see, I teach history and sometimes I get the feeling that my people think I am giving away secrets, you know, Hopi secrets." The Hopis don't want to lose anything anymore.

I said, "Yes, I do. That's why I talk about Private Property Week instead," and we laughed. And then I added, "And about the American Bicentennial." And the Hopi friend said with mock disbelief, "You mean it's been two hundred years already?" We laughed again.

Yes, it was two hundred years already and Private Property Week began that year of 1976 on Easter Sunday. As Charlie, a Navajo brother from the Four Corners area, would say, "Again?" without any mock disbelief at all.

Roxanne and I went to a Southwest Anthropological convention on a Friday to attend a session called "The Anthropologist and the Indian." Shirley, a Sioux scholar, was going to be speaking on Sioux linguistics, and we wanted to hear her. When we arrived at the conference room, a white man was speaking.

He was an archeologist from the University of Washington. He was telling about his and the university's efforts to dig up an old Indian village site in Washington. He used the word "recovery." The archeologist talked about the Federal government, the state government, and his own personal efforts to raise money to finance work on the site recovery.

Once in a while, he mentioned the Makah people who had lived there at the "site," who presently live at Neah Bay.

He said, "We had the Air National Guard fly the elders of the tribe down to the site." He said the Indians were amazed. When Roxanne and I had walked into the conference room and sat at the edge of the audience, the archeologist looked at us out of the corner of his eyes. "Of course, the younger Indians did not see exactly eye to eye with the elders," he said.

We decided to go get something to eat in the hotel dining room. After we had eaten and the waitress brought our check, we said, "This is a rip-off," and we walked out. The check was too high for a meager tasteless breakfast, and we weren't surreptitious at all as we walked away.

We went back to the conference room, still wanting to hear the Indian linguist speak. A woman was talking. This one was a linguist and she was also white. She was talking about preservation, and she said that there were several universities and organizations who were making the effort, funded by Federal and state money, of course. She mentioned a couple of Indian tribes, too, and her wish was that Indian languages be "preserved."

It was getting late in the day, and so we told Shirley, who was going to speak last, that we had to be leaving. "We wanted to hear you," we said, "but we have to go now." "That's okay," she said. "Goodluck then. You tell them good," we said. And she said, "Okay, thanks."

The next day, we did a session at the convention; we called it "Land, Water, Indians and Power." In the morning I had joked, "You can introduce me to the anthropologists as a wild, gut-eating savage heathen." And Roxanne laughed, saying, "Yeah, I'll tell them that you're a show and tell Indian. This is an Acoma Indian; he will show and tell." "I'll tell them, alright," I said, "and then I'll take it out and show it to them." Laughing, sometimes it's better to laugh.

When it was time for our session to begin, we put up our map of the Southwest, and then I wrote on the blackboard, "The Only Good Anthropologist," to remind myself. And to remind them. I didn't show and tell anything bizarre nor did I talk about Federal and state money for "recovery" and "preservation," and when I asked if there were any anthropologists in the session, we were not surprised there were none.

When I was about fourteen years old, I would walk back to the Indian boarding school on the way from the Sunday movies downtown, and I would pass by the Sanitary Laundry on Third Street. There was always a continual screech and an uneven hum of some sort of machinery in the dim shadows beyond the metal doors.

I didn't know why I always stopped and looked into the shadows, but I did. There was some sort of enchantment that absolutely drew me to the entrance of that warehouse-like building, but I didn't know what it was.

Years later, I was walking from the Indian Center on Valencia, up 18th Street. I was passing this building on the street when I heard the screech of a saw.

There was a high, piercing shrill of rapidly moving metal on wood. A burning smell hung in the air, acrid to the nostrils. And I reeled through the doorway and saw several men working at wood. Metal tables, machinery, woodburn odor, sawdust, vague light. The din of machinery, saws and drills, the edges of steel, and a bin of woodpieces, scrap. I walked over and chose one.

I remembered the wood sculpture I made one summer in southern Colorado. White pine, the feel of wood, the smell of the La Plata Mountains, the cool wind. Dreaming, I touched my fingers to the scrap of wood.

"I've worked here for eight years," a man in a canvas apron explained. "You get to do this easily." He zipped a piece of plywood into the saw blade so easily and neatly and quickly the wood cried against the steel. So easy and careful, he cringed with a smile. An older worker with steel rim glasses falling off his nose glared at me.

I reeled back into the street, the curved piece of wood retrieved from the bin clutched in my hands.

I don't think anybody noticed me hugging that piece of wood as I walked up 18th Street. I don't think anybody noticed the forests in me, the quiet footsteps I have taken in the Rockies and the Smokies. I don't think anybody knew the memory of touch in my hands upon the trunks of great firs and pines and spruces.

The smell of sap drove me careening over broken sidewalks, made me so silently angry my words refused to make any sense of that afternoon. The shadows of city buildings lurched into me.

Longing so hard for forests and clean and gentle mountain wind, I snuck up 18th Street, a memory of white pine needles cradled in my arms like a baby.

The stories, the songs, the words continue as they always have. Brown children are running around, laughing and yelling. An Indian man with a black cowboy hat sits behind an announcer's table. I'd shaken hands with him; he had broad hard hands and he smiled big. A Cree, who is a University professor, says, "He looks Crow. Yeah, that's what he reminds me of, a Crow man announcing an Indian rodeo in Montana."

The man is announcing the events of the Indian Culture Day program at the University. The Culture Day has gathered many people, Indians and non-Indians, from the community in northern California.

A while later, I meet an Acoma Pueblo woman. There were some Acoma pottery sitting on a display table, and I ask the woman behind it if she made the pottery. She shakes her head and points to an older woman sitting in a folding chair.

"Guwaadze," I say, holding out my hand. She shakes my hand, smiling, and says, "I'm fine, and how are you?" "Fine," I say and introduce myself as she is puzzled about who I am. "I guess I don't know you," she says, hearing my name, and then adds, "I still understand the language but sometimes I don't speak in Acoma." And we smiled together. "Yeah, sometimes, I don't either."

When I tell her who my mother and father are, she smiles in recognition and says, "Yes, I think I know who you are now. Your sisters are Linda and Rachel." "Hah uh," I say, "they're my sisters." And then she says, "I guess I'm sort of related to you then." "You are? Well, I'll be," I say. And then she explains that her father was related to my mother's first husband who passed away when my sisters were very young.

"Well, you know my mother married my father after that and I'm his son and that's why I'm an Ortiz," I say. "Yes," she says, "that's true, but I've been away from Acoma for thirty years. I go home sometimes but I've been away for a long time, and I don't know a lot of people anymore." I tell her that everyone is well at home. She smiles and I tell her I was to speak, read poetry and tell stories, maybe even sing, in a while. "Maybe that way you can catch up on the news," I say. She smiles.

A little girl with sparkling dark eyes keeps looking into my face as I buy a grapefruit soda pop from a Chicano student group. I smile and ask her what her name is. She giggles and runs away.

Before I speak, I go to the men's room. There are two little white kids in there. While I am washing my hands, the older one, who is about five years old, keeps lingering and then he asks, "You're a Indian aren't you?" I say, "Yep, I sure am." "I thought so," he says, "you know how I know?" The younger boy, about three, keeps tugging at his brother's hand. I smile and ask how he knows. He says, proudly, "Because you're wearing red and black. That's a Indian's colors." I look at my checkered shirt and then at them and say, "Yessir, you're perfectly right about that." And then they smile and leave.

While I am telling stories and poems, there are children running about in the gymnasium; they yell at the top of their voices, and they laugh. I think, The words are for them and the voices from all the generations are surrounding them and they become the sounds of running and laughing and shouting.

When I sing about Beauty Roanhorse, I watch the Crow announcer in the front row of chairs. He has a long angular face and his brown hands are folded together on his solar plexus and he pays thoughtful attention to the song. I think, He knows, he knows Beauty Roanhorse from somewhere, from the mountains, from a roadside in Arizona, some rodeo, some memory.

"I know that life is
I know that life is good
I know that life is good
I know that life is good."

When the song is finished, the muscles in the Indian man's face are set tensely for a moment and then he smiles, and I know that the words mean something, that the meaning of the stories, the songs, the words continue. They continue.